passing through veils

A Novel of Dread

John Harrison

WFP

WordFire Press

EBook ISBN: 978-1-68057-422-7
Trade Paperback ISBN: 978-1-68057-423-4
Dust Jacket Hardcover ISBN: 978-1-68057-424-1
Case Bind Hardcover ISBN: 978-1-68057-425-8
Library of Congress Control Number: 2022950777
Cover design by Janet McDonald
Cover artwork images by Adobe Stock
Kevin J. Anderson, Art Director
Published by
WordFire Press, LLC
PO Box 1840
Monument CO 80132
Kevin J. Anderson & Rebecca Moesta, Publishers
WordFire Press eBook Edition 2023
WordFire Press Trade Paperback Edition 2023
WordFire Press Hardcover Edition 2023
Printed in the USA
Join our WordFire Press Readers Group for
sneak previews, updates, new projects, and giveaways.
Sign up at wordfirepress.com

"Written with utter assurance, Passing Through Veils *is equal parts propulsive and prose. A ghost story tucked into a very human story; there's a scene in this book that made me jump. Graceful yet bold, rooted with room to breathe. It's even, at times, erotic. Strong women, strong men, clashing before strong backdrops of family, history, and the state of one's mind. John Harrison has written one of my favorite books of the year."*

—Josh Malerman, *New York Times* bestselling author of *Bird Box* and *Malorie*

"Harrison's fiction lingers long after you turn the final page. He's a born storyteller."

—Clive Barker, *New York Times* bestselling author

"Filmmaker John Harrison's novel, Passing Through Veils, *is as cinematic as you'd expect but also a real work of literary art, a romantic and unsettling blend of Daphne du Maurier and Shirley Jackson. A real pleasure to read."*

—Daniel Kraus, *New York Times* bestselling author of *The Living Dead*, *The Shape of Water*, and *Trollhunters*

For Leslie, Ian and Sidney, who always listen.

"Knowing your own darkness is the best method for dealing with the darkness of others."

—Carl Jung

prologue

Washington, DC

City of ghosts. For some, the Potomac sparkles with the lights of their monuments, their struggles memorialized, their accomplishments revered. For the rest, it's the purgatory of oblivion, the void of regret, where they linger, unfinished, unsettled.

And mightily pissed off.

There is a charming Federal-style brick townhouse on Reservoir Road near Wisconsin only a few blocks from Georgetown University where cathedrals of elms that are lush in summer and gothically spare in winter shade the streets. Within this home's late 19th Century walls are gracious family rooms with oak wainscoting and wide plank floors that murmur and sigh, while the upstairs is graced with two large bedrooms and ensuite baths enhanced by vintage mosaic tiling and claw foot tubs. The Master for Rebeca and Robert Wright, and another smaller one, a nursery, for their adored twelve-month-old son, Jack-Jack. On this hushed fall evening, the street is deserted of pedestrian traffic. Lights are coming on. Cocktails are being served, dinner is being set, people are watching Cronkite or MacNeil/Lehrer, or dressing for de rigueur political functions masquerading as charity events. Somewhere, Edith Piaf's tremulous soprano coaxes the pensive melody of "Autumn Leaves" into the breeze like a faraway dream. In a dark blue sedan parked down the street, the flare of a cigarette lighter briefly illuminates the hooded stare of a man who is looking up at the shadow crossing behind the sheers of a bedroom window.

Rebeca Wright sits at her marble-top vanity and rushes fingers through her thick but short raven hair making it look messy and chic at the same time. A Givenchy black dress hangs in wait on the closet door, but for now she's wearing nothing but a slip that clings to her gamine frame like second skin. Her olive complexion sets off her almond shaped ebony eyes staring back from the mirror with a catalog of emotion. Fatigue competing with sadness, resignation, and shame. Barely concealed just behind them is the reason.

Fear.

On her vanity, there's a beautifully hand-carved wooden box. A wedding gift from Rebeca's mother-in-law, a family keepsake passed down through several generations of Wright wives in which each left behind one singular, precious keepsake. A lock of a child's hair, a beloved poem, a treasured piece of jewelry, a humble shred of wedding veil, the memorial meaning of each long forgotten now, but all of which, Rebeca was assured, mystically retain their power to comfort and welcome each new member of the clan. Rebeca reaches inside for the memento she has added. A Walther PPK 32 caliber. Sleek, feminine, deadly. Her hand tightens around the grip as she drops the mag to check its load. In the mirror, the silhouette of a man approaches, and she can tell he's hiding something behind his back. She quickly returns the gun to the box and closes it before he sees.

"Happy Anniversary, darling," Robert says as he drapes a string of Tahitian black pearls around her neck. They must have cost a small fortune, she knows, but she doesn't look at them. Her eyes remain locked on her husband's gentle eyes in the mirror's reflection, and the fear and sadness of a moment ago dissolve into the hazy vacancy of passion.

"Make love to me," she whispers, pulling his hands down into her thighs. Her slip rides up easily as he leans over to press his lips to the back of her neck. She turns and starts tugging on the buttons of his tuxedo trousers, and while she struggles to free him he lifts her face to his. Their tongues tease as they watch each other get excited. And then they can't wait any longer. He picks her up and carries her to the bed. His mouth glides lightly over her throat, across her belly and into her hips. She grabs for the bedposts and gasps for air.

Downstairs on the stereo, Piaf continues to seek the essence of Johnny Mercer's classic ballad.

Afterward, while Robert quickly showers again, Rebeca waits in the parlor by the stereo, a vision in that simple but elegant Givenchy, listening to snapping wood in the fireplace accent Piaf's melancholy as it flirts with a distant siren outside. She's holding the cover of the LP, staring at it but not seeing it. There's a feral quality in her eyes provoked by the struggle between endorphins and adrenaline in her blood.

"It must be tonight," she tells herself, nervously smoothing a peeling corner of the album cover under which she's hidden the truth. *"It must end tonight."* She steels herself with a quick gulp of the Scotch that's been waiting by the turntable, but a child's laughter in the foyer distracts her. Jack-Jack, fresh from his bath, liberating himself from Nanny's embrace. He toddles unsteadily toward his mother, who picks him up and holds him close, breathing in the warm caramel scent of him as if for the very first time.

"You be a good boy for Nanny, Jack-Jack," Robert says as he glides down the stairs behind them.

"God, he's gorgeous," Rebeca thinks as he drapes a shawl over her shoulders. She wishes she could rush him back upstairs and ravish him again. But *It's Morning Again In America*, and after the somber

malaise of the previous decade, everyone is craving a little elegance, a little glamour, a little fun. It wouldn't do to be a grouch and not show up. Besides, this may be her best opportunity to end the nightmare. If she doesn't lose her nerve.

And is willing to suffer the consequences.

The antique mantel clock above the fireplace strikes eight with its Westminster chimes, and Rebeca hands Jack off to his dad, who squeezes a big laugh out of the child before "flying" him back to Nanny.

"We won't be late," he tells their very own Mary Poppins.

Rebeca leans in for one last Jack-Jack kiss and almost tears up when Nanny waves 'bye bye' with his tiny hand.

Outside, the street is still empty and quiet. Rebeca hangs on Robert's arm as they stroll down the sidewalk to their silver Mercedes 380SL Coupe convertible. He opens the passenger door for her but pauses when he sees the sedan parked down the street. Something about it puzzles him, as if he recognizes it but finds it strange to be here, at this time, in this neighborhood. The confusion is fleeting, though, and he shrugs it off.

Inside the car, Rebeca reaches into her clutch for a cigarette, and her face suddenly freezes. She pushes through the tissues, the lipstick, the compact, but it's not there. The Walther PPK. It's not in the clutch! *Shit!*

"Robert," she calls out as he crosses in front of the car, "I have to go back inside. I forgot something." She continues her futile dig into the clutch, but she knows it's not there. She left it upstairs. She pulls on the door handle. "I'll be right ba …"

The car lurches violently. She jerks her head up in time to see Robert's face smash into the driver's door window. His eyes meet hers, but he's not seeing her because he's already unconscious and starting to slide to the street.

"Robert!" she screams, stumbling out of the car. Her shawl catches on the latch and yanks her back, but she tugs violently and shreds it. She races around the Mercedes toward her husband, but something stops her. A child's cry. Little Jack, who has somehow climbed on to a table in the townhouse parlor and is reaching out to her as he crawls toward the open window there. And in that split second of her hesitation, Rebeca's fate is sealed.

A dark shadow sweeps up behind her and a man's hand yanks her chin back to bare her throat. The brilliant steel blade of a stiletto lashes out.

At the townhouse, Nanny dashes up behind Jack to prevent him from tumbling out the window. She clips the stereo turntable as she comes but pulls Jack away just in time. A dark blue sedan is disappearing around the corner on to Wisconsin Avenue. The street has gone unnaturally quiet. No breeze, no insects. Even the ambient din from DC across the Potomac has retreated into soundless shock. All that's left is the maddening glitch of "Autumn Leaves" floating out the Wright's windows to accompany Rebeca's gasping gurgle as she leans against the Mercedes coupe and clutches at her severed throat with bloody hands. The pearls around her neck are gone. She stares up at her son, and her mouth moves, but no sound comes out. And then, she slowly slumps over in a swamp of her own blood.

Inside the townhouse, the mantel clock chimes the quarter hour, while at the windows the only eyewitness to this crime is crying desperately, incapable of understanding what he's just seen. Nanny covers his eyes and pulls him away. His cries fade into the interior of the townhouse leaving only Piaf's desperate voice eerily mourning the falling leaves and her lost love over and over and over as the LP continues to skip.

chapter
one

Isn't there one door in this godforsaken place that will stay closed?" Sloane Fields kept pushing at a defiant cedar closet door until she heard the *snap* of its latch. But no sooner did she let go than it popped open again.

"It was built in 1896, Mother," came a voice from down the hall.

"When people were much smaller from the looks of things," Sloane said to herself. She could almost touch the low ceiling with her outstretched hand. "Doesn't it make you feel claustrophobic?"

"Makes me feel cozy," her daughter, Kathryn, replied as she came out of the master bedroom carrying an empty U-Haul box.

"I don't know why you couldn't have chosen a more fashionable neighborhood," Sloane mumbled as she followed her daughter down the narrow staircase.

Kathryn tried hard to subdue a long-suffering sigh as the two of them passed through the foyer into the parlor on their way to the kitchen. "What's more fashionable than Georgetown, Mother?"

The slap of their footsteps was harsh and echo-y in these uncarpeted rooms that, like all unfurnished spaces, felt smaller than they really were. The light streaming through the windows was dusty, pale, and dappled by the swaying elm trees outside. Carpenter tools and paint-drops littered the area. The place looked like a "before" site on one of those HGTV fixer-upper shows. Sloane kept her body tight and stiff as if she were afraid of being contaminated by this forsaken space with its chalky walls and grimy woodwork. *Of course,* Kathryn thought to herself, *Mother wouldn't have dared brave the streets of DC in anything but her very best.* Sloane Fields couldn't just drop in dressed in jeans. It was Neiman Marcus, head to toe, as if she were about to host an Embassy garden party instead of visiting her daughter's remodeling project. Even around the stables at the family's estate in Virginia, Kathryn's mother was always turned out. *"You never know who you'll run into,"* was her motto.

"Wanna beer?" Kathryn offered as she opened the refrigerator, a loudly humming Kitchen Aid that would have to be replaced soon.

"I'll stick to water," her mother said with a disapproving frown. She reached into a cabinet for the single glass Kathryn had there. The cabinet door kept swinging back open, but she knew her daughter was watching with an amused smile so she gave up trying to close it. An uncomfortable silence descended while they each sipped and avoided the other's stare.

"You don't think I can make it, do you?" Kathryn finally blurted after another of her mother's pointed sighs.

"I'm worried about you, that's all."

"You're not worried, Mother. You're afraid."

"Afraid?"

"Of losing control."

Sloane's eyes went dead as they always did when she was challenged. It was the sure harbinger of a calculated disengagement to follow, sometimes lasting an hour or two, sometimes even a day or more depending on the perceived offense, until the guilty party finally offered up groveling apologies often without even knowing why. Kathryn had watched her stepfather prostrate himself numerous times this way. He had ample reason to do so, of course, but no one, whether high and mighty or lowly and insignificant, was spared. Sloane Fields' cold shoulder did not discriminate. Kathryn, however, refused to cower. From an early age she never looked away from her mother's shark stare, and she could hold her breath longer, which pissed Sloane off even more.

"Shouldn't you be the one afraid of losing control?" she asked her daughter, cutting to the quick. This time Kathryn broke the stare first. Her mother had found the soft underbelly and poked it hard. The rest of the beer went down fast and sour.

"There's someone at the door," Kathryn said as she crushed the can and breezed off toward the foyer.

"I didn't hear anyone knock," Sloane said following her out of the kitchen, but Kathryn ignored her and threw open the front door, startling an attractive man in a bespoke gray suit who was reaching for the knocker.

"I … found the original blueprints," he said fumbling with several long brown mailing tubes under his left arm.

"Yes, Alex promised me you would. Come in, come in!"

"You're Kathryn?" he said stepping into the foyer and the laser beam of Sloane's stare. "Maybe I should have called first."

"No, no. I had a feeling you'd stop by," Kathryn said. "This is Jack Wright, Mother. His father used to own this townhouse." In her excitement, she snatched the mailing tubes from his arms without asking and hurried off to the parlor leaving Jack and Sloane staring at each other with awkward smiles.

"Look," Kathryn called out. "There's a fireplace behind this wall."

Sloane came into the parlor to find her daughter already perusing a cluster of plans spread out on plywood boards on top of hardware store sawhorses in the middle of the room. The renderings were slightly frayed, the parchment yellowed, but the lines were still clear, and the dimensions precise. They were a memoir of this home's conception.

"My father broke the place up," Jack said as he came to the doorway. "Rented out the first floor and moved upstairs. Not long after my mother died." He seemed reluctant to come any further, but his eyes remained riveted to the windows looking out to the street.

"Which was your room?" Kathryn chirped as she flipped through more of the architectural elevations, but Jack didn't answer. Had he heard her, or was he ignoring the question? Sloane turned to him with an expectant expression.

"I didn't grow up here," he said quietly and left out the rest.

Sensing she'd touched a nerve, Kathryn put her myopic enthusiasm on pause and came over to him. "Thanks for the trouble you've gone to," she said. "My contractor will find these plans really helpful."

"Enjoy yourself. It was a beautiful home once. At least that's what I've been told." He looked around the room with an expression Kathryn couldn't quite decipher. Was it nostalgic melancholy, or a kind of rueful suspicion?

"I hope you'll come back to see that I've done it justice."

For the first time Jack smiled, but he left it at that. He nodded politely to Sloane. "I'll see myself out."

Kathryn waited until he vanished out the door, then turned back to find her mother watching with raised eyebrows.

"Quite good looking, isn't he?" Sloane said.

"And very, very rich," Kathryn responded, knowing that would impress her mother more.

THE SKY WAS an angry mess and threatening rain when Kathryn accompanied Sloane across the street to her Jaguar XL.

"Wasn't there a murder in there? I seem to recall ..."

"Not in there," Kathryn replied. "On the street. Jack Wright's mother, in fact. A robbery. Right there where you're standing."

Her mother almost jumped, as if a puddle of blood still lingered under her shoes. Kathryn wanted to laugh. She couldn't help it. "It was over thirty-five years ago, Mother," she said barely suppressing a smile.

Sloane glanced back at the townhouse with a slight shiver. "It's like it's staring at us," she murmured.

"Just tell your friends it's almost in Virginia."

"*Almost* isn't there, darling." She slid into the Jag, closed the door and lowered the window. "Watch the drinking," she said. "And don't forget to take your meds." She offered a cheek which Kathryn dutifully, if lightly, kissed. She watched her mother drive off as heavy drops of rain started pelting her face. She closed her eyes and lifted her face toward the treetops that were now swaying with gathering winds. The rain felt good, cleansing. She was looking forward to that fresh damp smell that would follow when it stopped. She'd throw open all the windows of the townhouse and let the scent overwhelm the odors of paint and sawdust.

And then she felt someone staring at her.

She opened her eyes and looked around. No one was on the street. But she caught a glimpse of a woman's silhouette hiding behind some curtains in the bedroom window of the townhouse next to hers. She had to blink away fat raindrops cascading from her forehead, and when she looked again, no one was there. And that's when the skies opened up.

Back in her parlor, Kathryn gathered up one of the blueprints Jack Wright had brought and stepped into the center of the room. As she studied the elevations, she began spinning around, trying to divine the dimensions exactly as the original architect had intended. Walls and studs melted away then reassembled in a different configuration, revealing the way this room had been before Robert Wright, according to his son, altered it to create a small renter's apartment. Suddenly the room was bigger. Charming furniture began to appear in tasteful arrangements.

Muted color now graced the cream and taupe walls and ceiling, off-setting busy Orientals on the floor. The more Kathryn succumbed to this Private Idaho, the faster she turned, letting her imagination run rampant.

It's been waiting for me. This house. Waiting for me to bring it back to life.

Her smile turned into laughter, exhilarated and unrestrained, until suddenly she stopped. An embarrassed self-consciousness swept away her reverie, as if some lingering essence of Sloane Fields remained in the atmosphere to chastise her for feeling so free. Once again, Kathryn had a creepy sensation that someone might be watching her.

She had no way of knowing that she'd just been imagining a decor that closely resembled the way everything looked the night Rebeca Wright was murdered.

chapter
two

The Nabeyaki Udon from Harmony Café on M Street wasn't bad. It had arrived still steaming hot, and even though Kathryn had to slurp it out of a plastic take-out container instead of the traditional clay pot she'd be served at the restaurant, the noodles were firm and chewy, the veggies wonderfully crisp. Definitely worthy of the extra five-dollar tip she gave the delivery boy. She was sitting at a flea market card table in the kitchen with one of the architectural elevations Jack Wright had delivered, contemplating her good fortune. It was only a few months ago she was a hallucinating wreck confined to the psyche ward of George Washington University Hospital. No Nabeyaki Udon on the menu there, although the room was a comfortable if deliberately banal approximation of one you'd find at any Hampton Inn. A few jolts of electro-convulsive therapy and a continuing regimen of Risperidone, Lorazepam or Haloperidol, plus annoyingly intrusive conversations with Dr. Tami Frankle finally got Kathryn back on her wobbly feet.

And here she was. The first night in her new home, her very own Enchanted Castle. The utter quiet enveloped and mesmerized her. It was almost a sound in itself. She focused on the little interruptions. Each creak in the walls, each drip of a faucet in another room, each tiny whine at a windowpane when a breeze passed over the house. They weren't annoying, they were comforting. And then there were sounds she couldn't identify at all. Noises that could be … anything! The more she listened, the more amplified and specific they became. Especially the repetitive *clicking* coming from the foyer. Like a Morse code. *Click click click.* Pause. *Click click.* Pause. *Click click click.*

"It's a living thing, this house," she thought. *"Old and cranky, but still solid, still fit."* Worth whatever blood sweat and tears she would put into it. The things it must have seen and heard in its hundred plus years, the laughter, the anger, the intrigues and passions that must have seeped into these walls, embalmed beneath successive coats of paint and varnish, recorded in the scars on the flooring, preserved in the smells of its woodwork. This house was history incarnate for anyone willing to interpret the signs.

Click click click. Pause. *Click click.*

Just like the ballpoint pen in Dr. Frankle's hand as she unconsciously and repeatedly pressed the plunger while contemplating the most inexplicit way to draw Kathryn out.

"You're on a wonderful journey, Kate," Frankle had said at their appointment earlier, staring at Kathryn with those fatigued and watery eyes.

Click click click.

Didn't she realize how irritating it was?

"A journey of self-adventure, of self-discovery." Her maternal, soft-spoken manner could be calming or exasperating, depending on one's mood. Kathryn's was always unpredictable. Thus, Dr. Frankle's caution.

"I've asked you to stop calling me that," Kathryn moped. "I know it's difficult, especially since she won't."

"She?" Frankle asked even though she knew exactly who Kathryn was referring to.

"The Wicked Witch of the West. Just don't call me that, okay?

I'll never be the incarnation of Katherine Hepburn no matter how much my mother wishes it."

"And so you changed the spelling of your name," Frankle said.

We both know why I changed my name, Kathryn thought, *but let's not go there. Please. Not today.* "I want to be ordinary, okay? Plain-wrap and uncomplicated." She slowed her breathing as Frankle had taught her. "Except when I try not to be. And we know what happens then." Her eyes darted around the room to confirm what she meant.

"I take it this morning was a little intense."

"She couldn't get out of there fast enough."

"And how did that make you feel?"

Kathryn settled back on Frankle's stare. What a ridiculous and predictable question. *How do you think it made me feel, you clueless cow. Sorry. I meant 'you kind counselor.'* "Like it always does," Kathryn answered meekly. "Inadequate."

"And yet, a new house, a new job. Hardly what I'd call inadequate. Perhaps a good look in the mirror is called for."

Kathryn allowed herself to be buoyed by the encouragement until Frankle reached for a prescription pad and started scribbling.

"What's that?" Kathryn asked.

"Prolaxsis. I want you to try it. We'll start with ten milligrams. But we can bump it up if you feel you need it."

"Why do I need it at all?" Kathryn knew what it was. Classmates in law school used to pass them around before exams. Helped with the anxiety.

"You remember our agreement?" Frankle's stare was unyielding.

"Of course," Kathryn acquiesced.

"We don't want any more … episodes, do we?"

"God, no."

"Would you tell me if there had been?"

Click click click.

"Would you bring me back … here?" Kathryn whispered.

Frankle put her pen down and leaned forward to take Kathryn's hands. "Kathryn, no one wants you to come back here. Not I. Not your mother. No one. But it's up to you. You must take control. You're in charge of your own destiny now."

They never did get around to the real cause of her psychic break, and maybe they never would. Which was fine with Kathryn. It was easier to accept Dr. Frankle's insistence that, contrary to fictional accounts and talk-show analysis, the manic episode she experienced was more a surrender to toxic brain chemistry than the consequence of some repressed emotional trigger. The slow erosion of her reality grip resembled nothing so much as the inevitable sloughing of sunburnt skin, flake by atrophied flake, until all her insulation was gone and only a raw and itchy dermis of disconnected thoughts, horrific images and ensuing agitation remained. Coherence had fled the scene, and there was nothing left to do but submit to a higher authority. Drugs, electroshock, Dr. Frankle, and a six-month 'staycation' at GWU Psych.

But here she was now in her new home on a *journey of self-discovery*' and restoration, not only of this old townhouse but her own mind. She leaned back and closed her eyes, allowing a surge of satisfaction to wash over her. Frankle was right, goddammit. *I am not inadequate.*

Click click click.

Too regular. Too predictable. Not pipes contracting in the walls. Not old floorboards settling. Something moving. Inside this house.

Click click click. Pause. *Click click.*

Kathryn came out of the kitchen and listened intensely. It wasn't coming from the foyer. It sounded like it was coming from the parlor. She moved to the doorway and paused. Her heart was pounding. Could someone have gotten in? She stepped cautiously into the room. The space was dark and vague. But no one was there.

Click click click.

The window! A small bird, a sparrow, was pecking mindlessly at the glass. Trying to get her attention? Kathryn came up to it slowly, unthreateningly, fascinated by this weird, abnormal behavior. The sparrow finally saw her and their eyes met. But the bird didn't spook. It just sat there staring at her. Then it tapped some more. The same exact pattern. And when Kathryn didn't move or respond, it tapped again. Like it was signaling her.

Then, all of a sudden the little bird tensed up, its feathers rising like the fur of a cornered cat. It appeared to be looking past Kathryn into the room, seeing something it didn't like. In a flash, it leapt off the windowsill. Kathryn jerked back as its wings beat against the glass and pushed away into the night. She spun around to see what had startled the little thing. One of the pocket doors between the parlor and foyer was creeping out of its cocoon, so slowly as to be almost imperceptible, but definitely sliding forward as if being pushed from inside the wall.

"Hello? Is someone there?" Kathryn called out unable to think of anything else to say, but there was no answer. She came over to the door and tried pushing it back along its track into the wall. It wouldn't budge. In fact, it kept sliding forward. She pushed harder and harder, but the damn thing wouldn't retreat. It seemed to be fighting her, and winning, until all of a sudden it jumped out of her grip and skidded back into its sheath with a bang. Had she shoved it that hard?

"Shit," Kathryn muttered as she sucked chafed fingertips. For a long moment she glared at the wall where the door was now nestled. Then she stepped out to the foyer to check it from the other side. There was nothing unusual. *Just another door that wouldn't stay closed. Right?*

Kathryn's breathing finally slowed to a normal rhythm and she felt a flood of calm sweep back up her spine. But with it came a wave of fatigue that almost made her legs buckle. It had been a long day. The exhilaration of her new adventure competing with the stress of her mother's disdain and Dr. Frankle's mental hovering was exhausting. She turned off the lights and headed for the stairs.

Shedding clothes as she crossed the bedroom, Kathryn went into the bathroom and began throwing cold water on her face and down the back of her neck. She wanted to finish a chapter of the book she was reading before she turned off the lights and didn't want to fall asleep mid-paragraph. She picked up the bottle of Prolaxsis Dr. Frankle had prescribed, but stopped before opening it. Tomorrow was her first day in the new job. She needed to be sharp, needed to be clear and focused. She needed to be *on*. She hated the gummy way her meds made her feel in the morning. Besides, she was fine without them. In control. Master of her own destiny. An eight-hour drug holiday couldn't hurt surely. She put the bottle back down.

She was brushing her teeth when she thought she heard the laughter. And the music. She wasn't sure at first, but when she paused her electric toothbrush and held her breath along with a mouthful of toothpaste, she heard it for sure. A party. People laughing, and someone singing. A voice she thought she recognized.

She spit and rinsed and went back to the bedroom. The pill bottle trembled at the edge of the sink then tumbled to the floor and rolled behind the toilet bowl. Almost as if it had been pushed.

The source of the noise was hard to locate. From the bathroom, it had sounded like it was downstairs. But when she went to the doorway to listen it suddenly sounded like it was behind her. Maybe it was in the house next door. After all, these old townhouses practically shared walls with each other. As she came back across the room the music did get louder, and the closer she got to the wall the more distinct it became. She put her ear to the plaster. Yes. It was there. The house next door. It took her a second to recognize the melody, but then it came to her. *"Autumn Leaves."*

"Hello ... hello," she called out, knocking on the wall. "Could you keep it down? Hello? Please ... it's a little late." She hit the wall a little harder.

And the music suddenly stopped.

"Thank you," Kathryn said to herself and settled down to the mattress on the floor. She picked up the copy of *King's Oak* she'd been re-reading and started to renew her love affair with Anne Rivers Siddons. Maybe not the best choice considering Siddons' psychologically variegated, often ragged characters, but Kathryn had always found it somewhat cathartic to read herself into Siddons' stories.

Then the music started again. Like a defiant slap in the face.

"Hey!" Kathryn yelled banging on the wall again. "Hey! Turn the music down. Please." Whoever it was kept singing. *Why do I know that voice?*

"Please, I have to get up early tomorrow." Banging harder now. "My first day at work. Be considerate. Please!"

And just like that, the music stopped again. Kathryn lay there, expecting the music to start up again. What would she do then? March next door and start yelling? Call the cops? But the music didn't start up again, and Kathryn was so tired the words in her book were swimming on the page. So she put it aside, turned off the light and stared at the ceiling until her eyelids began to fall.

The music didn't return.

The *clicking* did.

three

Kathryn bolted up in bed. Groggy. Disoriented. Almost as if she were coming out of a nightmare. This was why she hated taking those damn antipsychotic meds. They helped her sleep all right, but the minute she stopped taking them, like last night, her dreams became more vivid, more surreal. It was as if all the emotions and anxieties muzzled by the meds were finally set loose, and the chaos of her now unrestrained synapses resulted in a surge of strange and disturbing narratives.

She glanced over at the wall where she heard that music last night. Or did she? Was it just a dream?

Click click click. Pause. *Click click.* Pause. *Click click click.*

That was no dream. That was downstairs!

She came out of her bedroom and paused at the top of the stairs to listen. There it was again, that light tapping. Coming from the parlor. She hugged the wall halfway down the stairs to get a better look. How did those pocket doors get closed?

Click click click.

Was it that bird again? Had it gotten in somehow? Gotten itself trapped behind those damned doors? And who closed them? Did she?

Kathryn padded across the foyer to the parlor and took a deep breath. She decided to rush into the room and close the doors behind her before the bird could escape. Then she'd dash to the windows, throw them open and hurry back out, sliding the doors closed again. With any luck the little thing would find its way out eventually, hopefully without dropping weight as it fled.

Like last night, though, the pocket door skidded away from her as soon as she touched it, and sunlight flooded into the foyer. There was a man in the middle of the room standing by that sawhorse table fitting together two pieces of crown molding that would eventually grace the upper walls of the room. He put down his little hammer as soon as he heard the pocket door slide.

"Seven o'clock. You said seven, right?" he said with a slightly chagrined tone.

"Yes, I did. Sorry, Russell. I didn't mean to startle you. Never heard you come in."

"Thought you'd left already."

"I've overslept. I'm gonna be late. Keep doing what you're doing. Just lock up when you leave."

"Will do."

"By the way, the previous owner stopped by yesterday with those blueprints I mentioned. They're in the kitchen."

"Great. I'll have a look."

Kathryn rushed back upstairs to the bathroom, hoping a quick cold shower followed by a triple espresso from Pâtisserie Poupon would sweep away the overnight cobwebs. If she hurried, she could still make it to the office on DuPont Circle by eight-thirty. But a few minutes later when she hurried out of the townhouse, she felt a tingle on the back of her skull, like the kiss of a gentle breeze barely sweeping over the hairs of her skin. Something unnatural about it made her turn to see if someone had snuck up on her and was literally breathing down her neck. There was no one, of course, but out of the corner of her eye she thought she saw that same silhouette staring down at her from an upstairs window of the townhouse next door. The townhouse where that music had been keeping her up. When Kathryn looked, though, the silhouette moved away quickly and a curtain dropped.

"Okay, fuck this," she muttered to herself. Taking a deep breath, she steeled her nerves, marched up to the townhouse's front door and knocked decisively. "Hello? Hello? Anyone home?" For a moment, nothing happened. The street was quiet. Nothing stirred. And her next-door townhouse just stood there, looming over her, insolent and challenging.

But then the heavy *crack* of a deadbolt made Kathryn jerk back. A moment later the door pulled open. Out stepped a stern middle-aged apron-clad woman who closed the door behind her and blocked the way. Kathryn's fleeting determination retreated behind the wall of her insecurity.

"Uh … hi, my name is Kathryn Fields. I'm your neighbor, just moved in next door, and I really hate to complain, but well, there was a party or something here last night, the voices were pretty loud, and someone was playing the radio or boom box, and my bedroom shares a wall with your house, and I just wanted to ask …"

"There was no party," the woman interrupted. "No music neither."

"Look, I don't mean to be rude. It's just that I'm starting a new job and …"

"Miss Dupree lives alone. And she don't listen to no music."

"Miss Dupree?"

"The woman what lives here."

"And you are?"

The woman stiffened. *Who are you and why should I tell you?* body language. "Maggie," she said. "The housekeeper."

"Then you're not here at night …"

"Not last night. My night off."

"Maybe Miss Dupree had some friends over? After you left?"

"Miss Dupree never talks to no one. Or listens to music, or nothin' else for that matter."

"But I heard it," Kathryn said and couldn't help thinking she was sounding like a whining child. "On the other side of the wall. It had to be coming from here."

"I told you, no music. She's deaf!"

Kathryn stepped away from the woman and stared up at the window where she saw that silhouette. Was the curtain moving again? Before she could challenge Maggie, the housekeeper stepped back through the door and closed it hard. The *thwum-mmpp* of the deadbolt put a blunt end to the conversation. Kathryn just stood there, confused and unsettled, embarrassed by her presumption but pissed, too, by the housekeeper's curt dismissal. She almost reached up to knock at the door again but then realized how late she really was now. She marched off across the street and forced herself not to glance back at the second story window. If she had, she'd have seen that silhouette hiding at the edge of the frame again, staring down.

As it turned out, Kathryn had to cool her heels in one of the small conference rooms of Brackenridge, Kelly and Levine until her best friend, Alexandra Gold, sauntered in a half hour late, suffering a massive hangover, courtesy of a raucous girls-only Women's Legal Council annual dinner. Still, in her silk Blazé Milano double-breasted blazer and matching gray slacks the woman exuded the kind of confidence only career suicides would confront. She had enough charisma to charm a cobra into surrendering its venom. Besides her looks, Alex combined knife-fight street smarts with a warm honey personality that made victims feel like they'd won while they bled out. No wonder she was being fast-tracked to a partnership and seven figures while barely settled into her middle thirties. Recruiters everywhere from the State Department to the alphabets competed to lure her away from the private sector. She always demurred, but she was too savvy to slam the door. She just wanted to make a "gusher of money" first.

"Gawd, what I'd give for an overcast day," she said with a mouthful of Texas as she came through the door and peered over her sunglasses at Kathryn. "Never challenge a girl from El Paso to a tequila contest."

"I take it your opponents conceded the fact," Kathryn laughed.

"We had a *come to Jesus* moment around two-thirty this morning. Two of 'em have already canceled a contract arbitration scheduled for this afternoon."

"Afraid you'd clean their clocks, no doubt."

"You said it, honey." She grabbed two Ethos bottles of water and chugged one. She led Kathryn out of the conference room and into the BK&L's tony corridors where thick carpeting and frosted glass walls muted the incessant commotion of associates, executive assistants, paralegals, and fixers, all on the make, all jockeying for partner access.

"Can't you just taste the testosterone in the air around here? We're lucky our girls aren't growing mustaches," Alex chortled as she polished off a second bottle of water. An earnest young associate fell in behind them desperately wanting her to look at something on the Surface tablet he was carrying, but Alex ignored him.

"It's okay to be nervous, right?" Kathryn whispered.

"About what? A bunch of middle-aged Peacocks trying to hang on to the wreckage?"

They turned a corner into Alex's corner office.

"Don't get me wrong. The women are worse than the men. Equal opportunity, right? But, honey, you're smarter than most of them, more charming than all of 'em. Hell, you've probably forgotten more than most of 'em ever knew."

She was right, of course. Kathryn had been a been a *one to watch* in college, the editor of Georgetown's Law Journal, recruited to Watson, Cohen, Daniels and Marbury, one of Philadelphia's elite white shoe firms, easily navigating the competitive gauntlet of first year associates until the gimlet gaze of octogenarian Wesley Daniels, the rain-maker himself, fell upon her, and she found herself traveling the world counseling him on international corporate cases with billion-dollar consequences. Her political insights and aggressive legal strategies went beyond the brief of her rank and caused no small amount of envy among her more punctilious colleagues. But Daniels enjoyed her iconoclasm and "fuck convention" attitude, and he rarely reined her in. Until, that is, the night in Tokyo a year ago when too much sake inspired a full-on shouting match with the Japanese Prime Minister over his refusal to acknowledge the national shame of Korean 'comfort women' during World War II. Banished by her mentor, Kathryn continued to drink heavily while flying back to Philly alone on the firm's private jet. When she became abusive and incoherent, the pilots made an unscheduled stop in Los Angeles to unload her. She assaulted one of the security guards who had the unfortunate duty of escorting her off the plane. She was in full psychotic break by the time police arrived. Doctors diagnosed mental and emotional exhaustion brought on by overwork and stress. Only her family's connections and Wesley Daniels' affection kept the incident out of the papers and Kathryn out of jail. She spent the next six months in the care of Dr. Tami Frankle at GWU Psych. Damaged goods. A great career, a partnership, possibly even a judgeship, crashed and burned.

As soon as she stepped into Alexandra Gold's office, Kathryn seized up. A vision of what could have been paralyzed her. The carpeting cost more than an average person's salary.

"Okay, Josh, what is it?" Alexandra said without looking up at the earnest young assistant who had followed them in.

"Senator Warren has called three times," he said offering the tablet. Alexandra groaned. Josh stiffened but carried on. "So has Senator Graham." A smaller voice.

"Christ on a cracker, *why don't they just call each other?* Who do they think I am? Condi Rice?"

"You missed your breakfast appointment with Tommy Truax about his Fed Court nomination …"

"He'll get over it," Alexandra said absently as she signed into her computer terminal.

"… and Anderson Cooper is on one."

This got her attention, and she quickly picked up the phone. "You're a pest, Andy, you know that?" she chirped. "Adorable, but a pest." She mouthed the words *"hates when I call him Andy"* to Kathryn who backed up slightly as if shy about over-hearing. Alexandra waved off her concern, set the phone on speaker and started to answer emails. Cooper's rapid-fire cadence could be heard pleading for a meeting to discuss an investigation he and his team were pursuing into a possible privacy hack at one of her biggest corporate clients. After a moment, she picked the phone handset back up and interrupted.

"Okay, okay, send your little chippy. Usual place. He's buying. But make sure he comes alone. I see anyone pretending to talk on an iPhone within a hundred yards and he can finish the ribs all by himself. Everything on background only. And remember, Amigo, my two favorite words are 'no comment.' Adios." She ended the call and nodded to Josh, who made a quick note on his tablet then slinked out of the office, closing the door behind him.

Kathryn couldn't help staring at the bookshelf of awards, tributes and photos. Alexandra with "W," Obama, various congressmen and diplomats, Arab princelings, even the Dark Lord himself, Vladimir Putin.

"Not bad for a hick from West Texas, huh?" Alex said while typing another email response.

"It's a little intimidating," Kathryn admitted as she sat across the desk from her friend.

Alex stopped what she was doing and leaned forward. "Look, hon, just remember that most of what goes on in this town can be filed under 'pretense and façade.' You keep that in mind and no one's gonna get over on you. C'mon, let's get you in harness."

Alexandra led Kathryn back through the maze of BK&L's corridors to a small office in the hinterlands. More of a monk's cell than an office. No windows, barely room to stand. But there was a shiny new nameplate by the door: Kathryn T. Fields, Esq. and on the desk, a stack of thick files.

"Farmer's Co-op versus Southern Pacific," Alex said leafing through them. "Wilson versus the City of Pittsburgh, and Schwartz versus Navy."

"And we are …?" she asked.

"Railroad, Pittsburgh, Navy, of course," Alex replied with a wry smile.

"Ah, the little guys."

Alex laughed as Kathryn came over to hug her. "I don't know how to thank you, Alex," she murmured.

"For what?"

"For rescuing me. For taking a chance. Getting me this job. Helping me close on that townhouse."

"Honey, you were the one that helped me get through law school. The job part was easy. As for the townhouse, well, you were the only one to make an offer on that dismal pile."

"Wait 'til you see it, Al. It's going to be wonderful. A total makeover. Just like me."

four

It was after dark when Kathryn finally left the offices of BK&L. She wasn't the last one out, though. Several younger associates were still huddled over their desks or in the library, eating take-out, staving off brain-fag with numerous cups of coffee. Jackets off, ties askew, blouses wrinkled and untucked, shoes off, sweating details of case law they'd be called upon to support their bosses' arguments for upcoming trials or negotiations. Kathryn didn't feel the need to remain with them, no need to share bonding miseries with exhausted, early-burn-out go-getters. *Been there, done that. With a vengeance.* She could easily do her homework back at the townhouse.

Georgetown was quiet when she turned off Wisconsin onto Reservoir Road. The warm glow of the street's faux gas lamps guided her way as autumn leaves swirled gently around her ankles. Somewhere a fireplace was scenting the air with burning maple. A tingling déjà vu suddenly swept over her. Not a hallucination. Not a vision. Just a pure, dizzying feeling that she'd been on this street before. Decades ago. Perhaps longer. Lots of external stimuli could set one of these daydreams off. A smell, a distant sound, a sudden change in light. They came on like a nervous shudder, and she always allowed herself to luxuriate in the romance of the moment. She loved the transcendence of it. When she was little, her mother used to call these reveries "Kate's woolgathering." As always, it was an ephemeral sensation, ending as abruptly as it began when she passed Miss Dupree's townhouse.

Kathryn paused to check for that silhouette in the second-floor window. No sign of it tonight. Only the dim glow of a table lamp inside backlighting closed curtains. Downstairs, dark as a tomb.

"Miss Dupree don't listen to no music. She's deaf!"

KATHRYN SLICED some cucumber chips while her Trader Joe's Lamb Vindaloo warmed up in the microwave. She settled in at the wobbly card table in the center of the room with a cold beer and the townhouse blueprints. She couldn't help imagining the elegance this home must have had, and what it could have again. She was thrilled with Russell's craftsmanship. He was a real find on Angie's List. He could be a bit of a pedant, especially when challenged about some of his restoration techniques, but he knew what he was talking about. And he was adamant that she not succumb to the romance of the fireplace they uncovered in the parlor until she'd had the gas company over to certify the safety of the log lighter pipe. After his lengthy lecture about the dangers of gas explosions, Kathryn felt duly cautioned. She couldn't wait for the downstairs to be finished so she could get the floor guys in to start the sanding and re-finishing while she moved Russell to the upstairs work.

She took the blueprints to her bedroom with her, mentally noting differences between the current structure and the architect's original intentions. The exhilaration of her new adventure emboldened and calmed her at the same time. For the first time in a long while she felt capable, confident, unsullied. "More than adequate," as Dr. Frankle would say.

Don't get cocky, her inner demons cautioned, but she couldn't help it. She hadn't felt this light in months. She was about to go into the bathroom to undress and brush her teeth when she noticed a dim light illuminating the window at the back of her bedroom, a window that over-looked the small backyard behind her town-house. Kathryn came over to close the blinds and saw that the light was coming from the garden next door where Miss Dupree, in her nightgown, was watering her flowerbeds. The old woman was tiny, five foot if that, with wispy unkempt hair that might have been red once but was now a dull rust color. A stiff breeze would have knocked her reedy body over. She looked like a ghost, or perhaps an ancient witch tending to her Belladonna at ten at night.

Kathryn couldn't help herself. She pushed open her window and leaned out. "Hi. Hello!" Then louder, "How you doing, Miss Dupree?"

The old woman barely moved.

"Your flowers look like shit, Miss Dupree," Kathryn called out, louder still, but the woman didn't react. She just stood there like a lawn ornament, pouring water on a bed of Chrysanthemum bushes. Kathryn gave up, pulled herself back inside and closed the window. *Miss Dupree don't listen to no music. She's deaf!*

Around midnight, Kathryn's eyes began to blur. She was in bed, in her pajamas, trying to study a brief about Ellen (née Alan) Schwartz who was suing the US Navy for medical coverage to complete her transition. Instead, she was distracted by fluffy pre-sleep, free-association images drifting aimlessly across her mind. Childhood memories of dressage competitions gave way to teenage tumbles in the family stables with awkward boyfriends that then morphed into the later, overheated ministrations of a more experienced lover, accompanied by mutating and dissonant melody loops from BK&L's elevator musak. Until finally one tune came to dominate. *Autumn Leaves.* A tremulous female voice, floating far away in the back of her mind. Or was it?

Kathryn's drowsiness quickly evaporated and her head jerked up. The music wasn't in her mind. It was behind the walls. Coming from the same spot as the night before. The wall connecting her townhouse with Miss Dupree's. She hopped out of bed and pressed her ear to the plaster. No doubt about it, that's where the music was coming from.

"Miss Dupree … Miss Dupree … please!" Kathryn cried out, slapping the wall. "Miss Dupree … please, this is so unfair. I can't get any sleep."

The music evaporated. Like the doppler effect of a train whistle, it just faded away, modulating in half-tones, lower and lower, until it dwindled into silence. Kathryn glared at the wall. Had Miss Dupree picked up the radio or boombox or whatever it was and moved to another room? Deaf old Miss Dupree? What kind of bullshit was this? Maybe it was Maggie, that Mrs. Danvers of a housekeeper. Maybe she had a room on the other side of this wall. Kathryn promised herself that she'd confront the sour crone first thing in the morning.

And that's when the music started again. Defiantly louder this time. A *'fuck you'* volume.

Kathryn pounded on the wall. "Turn that music down, goddammit! Miss Dupree, Maggie, whoever, if you don't turn that noise off, I'm calling the police." She was so angry she never noticed her breath condensing in little puffs in front of her mouth. But she felt the cold. The room seemed suddenly freezing.

Kathryn pounded the wall again, harder, and this time her palm cracked the plaster. She jumped back in shock. *"Did I really hit it that hard?"* A strange *hiss* leaked out of the seam in a rush, a mournful shriek that shredded Kathryn's nerves like a feedback screech from a high school PA system. Something flew out at her, brushing against her cheek as it passed. Her hands flailed spastically in front of her face and she stumbled away. When she looked back, she saw what it was. A large and stunning black butterfly with scarlet markings like lightning bolts on its wings. It was now perched at the foot of her bed, gently fanning the air, just sitting there as if staring at her. Kathryn turned back to the wall and ran a fingertip down the crack that appeared too thin for the creature to have slipped through. Had it really come from in there?

The music was gone, and when she looked back to her bed, so was the butterfly.

RUSSELL ARRIVED JUST BEFORE seven AM, a thirty-two-ounce Dunkin' coffee in one hand, a box of their famous donut holes in the other. Enough sugar and caffeine to power through the morning's work. Kathryn was already awake and waiting to divert him to her bedroom and the crack in the wall. After conferring over the blueprints Jack Wright had brought, they decided the wall had to be a relatively recent addition. Besides, Russell said, it was dry wall, not the lath-and-plaster of the original construction.

"So why would someone put a wall in front of a wall?" she wondered.

"You see it all the time in old places like this," Russell sighed. "People don't like something, they just cover it over." It didn't take him long to smash through the plasterboard and pull huge chunks away to reveal what was on the other side.

"Whad'ya know?" he said as he swung a flashlight beam into the darkness. There was a small dressing area hidden there. "Weird, huh? But then, I found a whole bathroom in a wall once. Plumbing still worked and everything. Guy even left a razor in the cabinet."

Kathryn wasn't listening to him. She was fascinated by the dusty marble-top vanity with its Queen Anne-style mirror and the delicate things in front of it. Perfumes, creams and powders, a sterling silver hairbrush. Neat. Orderly. Everything preserved almost like a shrine. Hanging on the wall was a gorgeous black dress. Kathryn recognized it immediately as Givenchy.

"There's your music," Russell said as he aimed the flashlight beam at an old Zenith radio next to the mirror. He leaned down and sprayed the wall with the light. "Huh," he added.

"What?"

He straightened up and showed her what he was holding. The power cord of the radio. "Unplugged," he shrugged.

"But I heard it. The music. It was coming from in here. I heard it."

Russell shrugged again and dropped the cord. "Better get my vac. Clean up this mess." He left her there staring at the unplugged cord in confusion.

"I heard it," she reiterated and leaned down to plug the radio back in. All of a sudden, it was on. Blasting Kendrick Lamar's "How Much a Dollar Cost."

She grabbed the radio and switched it off. She was now thoroughly freaked. But then she noticed the edge of a beautifully carved antique box partially hidden behind the mirror. She picked it up and the latch snapped open on its own. Curiosity triumphed. There were small mementos inside, a lock of a child's hair wrapped in tissue, a brief poem on yellowed paper, a shred of wedding veil sealed in a plastic bag, a small broach that must have had sentimental value because it looked more like Target costume-jewelry than even Kay or Jared. All resting atop a crinkled photograph of a stunning young woman with a thin, androgynous figure, like a fashion model. Short black hair that enhanced a perfectly symmetrical face, dominated by a strong jaw and wide-set almond eyes. Wearing that little black dress. Arm in arm with a handsome man in a tuxedo. But the picture was torn. And a piece of someone else's shoulder at the ragged edge suggested the tear had been deliberate and abrupt, as if someone had wanted to remove the person standing next to the woman on the other side.

Kathryn was mesmerized by the woman's penetrating gaze.

Straight into camera with a wariness in the eyes that felt somehow disconnected from the smile and body language. Their inky intensity was a vortex. Kathryn suddenly felt like a voyeur, like she had stumbled upon a private moment and that stare was a warning. Or was it an enticement? She quickly gathered up the mementos and the photograph and was about to replace them in the box when she noticed something else.

A gun. Hidden at the bottom of the box under a black velvet cloth. She couldn't resist picking it up. Although it was sleek and almost feminine, it had weight. It felt substantial.

It felt lethal.

chapter
five

As Kathryn hurried down Reservoir Road to her Metro stop at Wisconsin and Q, she almost ran headlong into Miss Dupree and her housekeeper, Maggie, out for the old lady's morning constitutional. She didn't recognize them at first since they were both bundled up against a fall morning chill, and she, preoccupied by those items she found behind the false wall in her bedroom, was motoring ahead oblivious to her surroundings.

It was the voice she heard in passing that made her stop.

"You look like her," it said.

"I'm sorry?" Kathryn responded, turning to them abruptly.

The two women stopped and Maggie looked back at her.

"She said something to me. That I look like someone," Kathryn said.

Before Maggie could answer, Miss Dupree stepped forward.

"Rebeca," she said pointing to Kathryn's townhouse. "She lived there."

"She can read lips," Maggie said answering Kathryn's question before she could ask it. Then she took Miss Dupree's arm, and the two of them turned back the way they were going.

"Excuse me, Miss Dupree," Kathryn called out, chasing after

them. Maggie gently stopped Miss Dupree again and turned her around. "You knew her? Rebeca Wright. You knew her?"

"She was murdered," Miss Dupree said. "Right where you're standing."

"You saw it? You saw what happened the night she died?" Kathryn enunciated every word, adding gestures in a kind of spontaneous, unthinking sign language as if speaking to a child.

The old woman glared dismissively. "Just the boy," she said pointing to Kathryn's townhouse again. "In the window there. He saw it all."

And with that, she turned away and continued down the sidewalk toward her own home, Maggie in tow, leaving Kathryn agape and uncomfortable, on the very spot where Rebeca Wright died.

NEWS of her murder made the front page of Washington Post on November 1, 1984. The coroner approximated time of death to be eight-fifteen PM since the nanny remembered the mantel clock chiming the hour just as *"the Missus and her husband"* left the house. Her notoriety as a former fashion supermodel and her story-book wedding to Robert Wright, one of the city's most eligible bachelors insured that this 'tragedy' would capture the public's imagination for a few days at least, and far longer than run-of-the-mill homicides of ordinary folk, which in this city were the province of the routine. There seemed to be no doubt that Robert and Rebeca Wright had been victims of a vicious mugging and robbery. He had been beaten into a coma for which he had to be hospitalized, his wallet taken and never recovered. She had been murdered while apparently rushing to his aid then fighting off the attempt to steal her pearl necklace. But since there had been no witnesses to the actual attack and no suspects, and after weeks of dwindling leads and public ennui, the case lost its 'redball' status and was soon demoted to the police's Open-Unsolved Unit of cold cases where it languished ever since. News items about the murder suffered a similar fate as fresher outrages soon overwhelmed it.

After about an hour in the library of BK&L that morning, Kathryn gave up the search for anything new or provocative about the case.

In the interests of full disclosure Kathryn had been made aware of the murder before she bought the townhouse on Reservoir Road, of course, but she hadn't given it much thought then. She was too wrapped up in her own issues, her 'escape' from the purgatory of GWU Psych, her new job, her need to *focus*. Still, finding that walled up vanity and the mementos Rebeca, or someone, left behind, goaded her curiosity. She warned herself not to obsess. This was a perilous tendency, according to her mother, Dr. Frankle, and even her best friend, Alex. Now was not the time to get manic about … anything. Still, the hour she'd allowed herself to scour internet archives for articles about Rebeca's murder left her feeling empty. Her sense of justice was offended, but something else was tugging at her, too, something she couldn't yet define.

During her lunch hour, she decided to scratch the itch.

It only took ten minutes to walk from her office down New Hampshire Avenue to the Ritz Carlton where the trendy Equinox Sports Club was located. As soon as she stepped through the doors, though, she regretted her decision. It was gleaming and unnaturally quiet. Decor was functional but stylish. The color scheme was a coordinated blend of beiges and sands creating an innocuous monochromatic effect. Apparently the movers and shakers of the nation's business took their fitness very seriously and tolerated little distraction. Mobile phones were forbidden by signage everywhere, and conversations were encouraged to be sotto voce, if at all. Arrays of TV monitors hanging from the ceiling like electronic stalactites displayed silent broadcasts of twenty-four-hour business, news and sports for which the audio could only be accessed via Blue Tooth headphones. Yoga and Pilates classes of sweaty and tortured hard bodies were confined behind glass walls where the grunts and groans demanded by drill-sergeant instructors could be politely muffled. There were attendants and personal trainers everywhere, and the bang of free-weights and fitness machines, the incessant whir of treadmills, spin cycles, and ellipticals was moderated by the constant drone of Spotify playlists of hundred-beat-per minute dance tunes curated by remote sadists to ensure bodies remained in motion not at rest. Sight and sound merged into a vertiginous throb that insulated this place from the rest of the world. It was a sanctum for focusing one's aggression.

And the sanctum sanctorum was a boxing area at the back of the club with two rings and enough training gear around them to exhaust Floyd Mayweather. Kathryn parked herself by a corner and tried to be to be inconspicuous, but she couldn't help being transfixed by the violence of glistening hyper-toned male and female physiques pummeling bags, pads, or each other. The attendant she'd spoken to a moment ago crossed the room and interrupted a sparring session between a trainer and his client, who spit out his mouthpiece, pulled off his headgear and turned to her. Jack Wright, the handsome guy who delivered blueprints to her townhouse the other day.

"Sorry to make you come all the way over here," he said to her as he jumped down from the ring. "Sean charges me a fortune for these sessions. No cancelations allowed."

"No prob," she smiled and struggled to keep her eyes locked on his instead of roaming all over his well-maintained anatomy.

"We'd just get interrupted at my office, and I'm not real comfortable visiting Dad's," he paused, "I mean *your* place."

"I understand."

He gestured to a small juice bar behind them. "What can I get you?"

"Uh … apple juice would do it. Thanks."

She sat at a high table and now took the opportunity to indulge a visual meander while he wasn't looking. He almost caught her when he turned back with her juice and some ugly looking smoothie that must have been made with weeds.

"I'm impressed," she said looking back toward the boxing rings.

"You like boxing?"

"I'm ashamed to admit I can never stop watching the TV if I stumble upon a fight. There's something elemental about it, I guess, that appeals to me."

"Ah, a kindred spirit," he said, toasting her with his smoothie. "So, how's the labor of love coming?"

"Labor of lunacy, depending on who you're talking to."

"Yeah, I got the impression your mother wasn't very enthusiastic."

Kathryn couldn't help wincing. "She thinks I'm running away," she said without thinking.

"From what?" His voice was softer and, Kathryn thought, a little too intimate all of a sudden. It took her a moment to answer.

"From her," she finally replied.

"Are you?"

His stare was sticky. She desperately wanted to change the subject. "I prefer to think of it as my declaration of independence."

"Good answer. Never look back," he sucked on his smoothie and smiled.

And she liked it. His smile and his attitude. But then she remembered why she was here. She reached for her purse.

"I didn't mean to pry. It, the box, it just popped open. Nothing too valuable inside, I don't think. Just mementos. Some brushes, some old perfumes. The dress is stunning though. I thought you'd want to know. Especially about this." She pulled out the torn photo she'd discovered. "Your mother, I assume."

She laid it down and pushed it toward him, but his expression darkened instantly, and she was sure he recoiled a little.

"Oh, god. This was a mistake," she whispered.

"No, no it's okay," he said. He tried smiling again, but it was strained. "Look, I really don't care what you do with it." He turned the photo over and pushed it back. Kathryn could have sworn his hand was trembling. "In fact, just throw it all out," he shrugged. "Give the dress away. Whatever you like."

"I'm sorry. I didn't mean to upset you." She was sure the heat rising in her cheeks had to be noticeable.

"You couldn't possibly." He was trying to seem blasé but it came off as abrupt and rude instead. He turned away and sucked on his straw that reached the bottom of the cup with a loud slurp. The silence that followed was awful. Fortunately, a ringside bell clanged and interrupted it, and someone's voice called out to Jack to quit flirting and get his ass back to work.

"Saved by the bell, huh?" he said.

"And I'd better get back to the office." She offered a hand, and he took it graciously, but it was an indifferent courtesy.

"Don't work so hard," he said backing up to toss his smoothie cup in the trash and return to the ring. She watched him go. Why had she come here? She'd only made a damn fool of herself. She hurried away to the door, and then the worm of indignation turned. *What the hell?* she thought. *Why am I feeling like such an inadequate ass? I am not inadequate. I was just trying to do something nice. Why wouldn't he want to know what I found?* She turned around and was about to march back and get in his face, but she stopped when she saw him slamming fists into a heavy bag so hard the trainer holding it staggered. There could only be one way to describe his expression. Enraged.

She hurried back up New Hampshire toward DuPont Circle, a forced-march stride, avoiding eye contact, until someone grabbed her arm from behind and spun her around. Her eyes flared with panic and hostility until she recognized who had assaulted her.

"Jesus," Jack said slightly out of breath. "You could win a marathon with that pace. I've been calling after you for two blocks."

"I didn't hear you."

"I gathered that."

Both were suddenly aware of suspicious stares beating down on them. Here was a half-naked sweaty man, admittedly a hunk but still, yanking a pretty woman by the arm when she wouldn't answer him. Were those smart phones aiming at them? He realized he was still holding on to her and abruptly let go.

"Look, I was rude back there. Too much adrenaline or something. I apologize. Really. Sometimes I'd rather just forget my family history, and I hate when I'm reminded of it. It's like I should feel, I don't know, *something* about what happened. But I don't. I was only a year old when she died. She's just a story in old newspapers, that's all. And then that pisses me off even more. Makes me feel helpless, you know? But then, how *would* you know? Right? You were just being considerate. And I was being a jerk. No excuse. I'm really sorry."

He was talking so fast Kathryn couldn't keep up. She needed him to relax, so she took his hand. "You don't have to explain anything to me. I presumed something I shouldn't have. I intruded where I had no business."

"No, there was no excuse for that kind of behavior."

Their body language dispersed the tension that had been gathering around them. *Move on, nothing to see here.* Stares diverted, mobile phones returned to pockets, purses, or ears.

"You have to let me make it up to you," Jack said.

"It's okay, really."

"What are you doing tonight?"

"You mean like *tonight* tonight?

"There's a charity thing I have to attend, my uncle's thing, and I would feel so much more charitable if you'd come with me."

Kathryn was starting to feel short of breath. She wasn't ready for this. "I don't know. It's a school night. Maybe a rain check?" A convenient dodge, she hoped.

Didn't work. "People miss a lot of life collecting rain checks," he said. "So, if you don't want that cop across the street coming over to ask if this sweaty guy wearing nothing but gym shorts and flip flops is bothering you, you better say yes." And there was that smile again. Nothing strained about it this time. Just genuine and very attractive charm. Her hesitancy was all the answer he required. "Good. I'll pick you up at seven thirty." And before she could object, he spun around and started jogging back toward Equinox. He didn't even give her a chance to ask what she should wear.

THE REST of the afternoon passed in a blur. No matter how much Kathryn tried to concentrate on her work, case details became co-mingled. Coworkers' questions were met with uninspired answers. She even made the mistake of confusing plaintiffs' names in one of her memos and was ready to send it to Alex when she caught the error at the last moment. Instead, she sent a brief note complaining of "cramps" and said she'd finish up at home, to which Alex immediately replied with a sympathetic emoji face.

Work didn't get any easier at home, and Russell's hammering in the parlor didn't help. All she could think about was how to get out of going with Jack Wright to his charity thing. But then, *why shouldn't I go,* she argued with herself? She used to own evenings like this with her charm, her wit, her flirtatious navigation. She could quickly assess any room and weave a path effortlessly to the center of it. Surely those skills hadn't atrophied completely. Or had they? When did she lose her spirited audacity? Did she ever really have it? Maybe it was it just a brittle shield she'd contrived, a counterfeit persona she had assumed to camouflage her insecurity, a masquerade to hide the shame she thought she'd banished to oblivion. What would Dr. Frankle say about that? Kathryn was sure she knew what her mother would say.

It was almost six in the evening when she finally called a time-out to this internal debate and decided her vacillating was merely a way of avoiding saying no to Jack. She really did want to go. *Fuck it! So what if it's a disaster?* Expectations would be low anyway. No one expected to see Kathryn version 1.0. That woman didn't exist anymore. It was time to see if anyone could be interested in the update. She sent Russell home, grabbed a beer from the fridge and raced upstairs to take a quick shower in cold water to jump-start her heart rate. She caught sight of herself naked and dripping in the mirror. What was she going to wear? Hadn't thought of that. All she had in her closet were inoffensive skirts, blouses and sensible shoes.

She searched the bathroom for the bottle of meds Dr. Frankle prescribed. It took her a minute to find it wedged between the toilet and the wall as if it were hiding there. She ripped off the safety foil and downed one with beer to calm her nerves. And then, she took another. On an empty stomach she hoped a wave of calm would arrive more quickly.

That's when she remembered Rebeca's black dress hanging next to that discovered vanity. Russell had torn away most of the false wall but left the little shrine intact. And there it was. Givenchy. Simple and understated. Sexy but not exhibitionist. Glamour without ostentation. But would it fit?

Only one way to find out.

What happened next was so improbable that she refused to accept it even much later as she clung to a narrative that depended on reason not what really happened. Because the next few moments began a descent into a kind of delirium from which she wouldn't soon escape.

As soon as she put on the dress she felt light-headed. It fit her like second skin, not a bulge or sag anywhere. She backed into the room and spun around to check all the angles in the vanity's mirror. She felt lovely, feminine, alluring. She hadn't looked this good in months and was almost embarrassed to be so impressed with herself, but the longer she looked the faster her self-doubt evaporated. The dress made her feel confident, even cocky. Kathryn 2.0 was hot, dammit!

That's when she saw the butterfly. In the mirror's reflection. Sitting calmly on the windowsill behind her, its scarlet-decorated wings undulating gracefully. But when Kathryn turned, it was gone. She looked around the room for it, but it had vanished.

Somewhere someone started singing. *Autumn Leaves.*

Kathryn gasped when she recognized it and a surge of anger swept over her. Her first instinct was to pound on the wall and yell at Miss Dupree. But this time there was no doubt where it was coming from. It was *in this house.* Downstairs.

She paused at her bedroom door, leaning close to confirm her suspicion. No question about it, the music was floating up the stairs from the parlor. She turned the doorknob as silently as she could to let the sound drift in through a thin crack. It wasn't just music. It was conversation, and laughter, and the sound of ice cubes clinking in cocktail glasses. Kathryn was sure she could smell cigarette smoke. She pulled the door open further and became suddenly paralyzed. There was expensive furniture where none had been before. There was art on the walls. There were thick oriental runners on the polished wood floor. The light from sconces that weren't there before was dim and foggy, but all of Kathryn's senses were instantly raw and hyperbolized. Her eyesight was 4K, her hearing was Dolby 7.1. Even her skin sensed a surreal pressure in the atmosphere. She padded to the stairs and looked down to see more furniture, more artwork. There was a glorious arrangement of gardenias on the antique console by the front door. The foyer was now tiled in a classic tuxedo pattern, and shadows from the parlor were sliding across it. She tried angling her view to see who was in there but like the rest of the home now the light was gauzy and vaporous. Kathryn couldn't make out what was being said. The conversations were flanged and harmonized into a kind of music all their own.

Everything seemed like it was happening behind a veil. Kathryn felt high all of a sudden. *Could those meds be kicking in this fast?*

"It's not fair, you know."

The man's whisper was so close to her ear that she swatted at it as if it were some pesky mosquito. He was right behind her, the man in the photograph she'd found in the memento box, the one with his arm around Rebeca Wright. Half his face was obscured in the dark, but there was no doubt. The narrow, chiseled face and high cheekbone, the dark eyebrow and full lashes. An utterly masculine, patrician face. Hard and remote except for his eyes which were riveting.

"The way you look, it's just not fair," she heard him say as he floated toward her. The shimmer of his tuxedo's notch lapels was mesmerizing. The smoke from his cigarette drifted lazily around his face, and the hand in his pocket kept opening and closing what sounded like one of those old-fashioned Zippo flint-wheel lighters.

Click click click.

"You shouldn't be allowed to make me feel this way." His voice was barely a murmur. Kathryn couldn't tell whether she saw his lips move or if his voice was only in her mind, but when he reached out to caress her face, his hands were so cold they stung. And when he leaned in to kiss her his lips felt viscous and gummy.

"What are you doing?" she hissed, trying to keep her voice from quivering.

"C'mon, darling. Let's be naughty. No one will know." His voice seeped into her mind as he tried to pull her back into the bedroom.

She batted away his arms. *Why couldn't she see the rest of his face?* Something fetid wafted toward her and she felt faint. A wave of terror made her stomach clench but not because of the hallucination standing in front of her, because she was now terrified of her own mind.

"I'm going insane," she said so softly she thought he wouldn't hear her. But he did.

"How do you think *I* feel? You'd be enough to drive Apollo mad."

And now his hands were on her again, caressing her breasts, pushing up her skirt as he tried again to pull her back to the bedroom. And that's when the light finally caught the other side of his face. She almost screamed. It was pale and featureless, torn and jagged down the side with a giant scar. The skin of the cheek drooped into a sinister sneer by the lip and the eye was a blank hole of nothing, just endless black. Kathryn shoved him aside, and was startled by how insubstantial he seemed. It was like pushing away a window sheer. She rushed into her bedroom and slammed the door. Her heart was racing and her breathing was shallow.

It's the meds, she insisted to herself. *I shouldn't have taken both those pills. I'm having a bad reaction.* She took a deep breath, closed her eyes and listened. The music was gone. So was the chatter. *Gotta talk to Frankle about moderating my dose.* Another deep breath, and she slowly opened the door again. The hallucination had evaporated. Not a trace of the furniture or the art or the carpet was left.

She sat back down at the vanity and tried to compose herself. *Get a grip, girl,* she said to her reflection, even managing a little chuckle. *Just another brain fart.* She sounded like she believed it. She had to believe it. Another deep breath. Back to reality. A touch of make-up, delicately applied, maybe pull back the hair, a good dose of Visine and she'd be presentable, maybe even attractive. She shook her head to dispel any lingering imagery from a moment ago. *Foolish girl. Just because you haven't been on a date in months, your goddamn nerves start freaking out? Don't be such a loser.*

She reached for one of the perfume bottles that Rebeca had left by the mirror. Chanel. Classic and subtle. Just the thing. She put a dot on her wrist.

The mirror cracked.

Kathryn jerked.

The glass cracked again, shattering her reflection into a Cubist portrait. She was too stunned to move. It wasn't her face staring back at her any longer. It was Rebeca Wright's, fragmented into bizarre geometric shards. Kathryn lurched back and threw her hands out defensively toward the mirror. Not to shield her face from breaking glass but to ward off the incubus on the other side. When she looked back, Rebeca was gone. Her own face stared back with slack-jawed horror.

And then her neck opened up. A thin red line at first, leaking blood and viscera as the jagged wound split wider and wider, exposing muscle and tissue. Kathryn gagged and grabbed at her throat. She leapt to her feet and stared down at her hands. No sign of blood or skin.

The world went black.

And she went to the floor.

chapter
six

A face loomed over her, blocking the bedside lamp like a lunar eclipse, the head enveloped in a bronze corona Kathryn couldn't decide was angelic or demonic. Her own head throbbed slightly but she wasn't disoriented. She knew exactly where she was. On her own bed. How she got there was the question.

"What happened?" she whispered.

"I think you must have fainted." It was unmistakably Jack's voice. That same soft, intimate slightly unsettling tone he'd used at Equinox. "I came to pick you up. Your front door was open."

"Really?" She was sure she had locked it when she got home from work.

"I thought I heard something fall up here, but you wouldn't answer me when I called out to see if everything was all right. I didn't mean to intrude."

"No, I'm glad you did, I guess."

"I found you on the floor. Over there." He gestured with his head toward the vanity and that cracked mirror but he didn't look at them. "Here, drink this." He helped her sit up and held the back of her neck while she sipped the glass of water he was holding. He was gentle and his expression was reassuring.

"I'm all right," she said. "Just crazy busy at work, and I forgot to eat. I'm fine. Really." She pushed her way to the edge of the bed and straightened up to make the point. "I'm sorry you had to find me like that. I've ruined your evening, haven't I?"

"Not at all. The reception isn't until eight-thirty, so I was going to try talking you into having a quick drink beforehand."

"Maybe we should forgo that part." She tried to laugh but it was weak.

"There will be plenty of food where we're going. You still want to go?"

"You still want such a fragile date hanging on your arm all night?"

"Would be the only thing making it tolerable," he smiled, that genuine, coaxing smile. "Think you can remain conscious 'til we get there?" he joked.

"Just give me a moment. I need to put myself back together a bit."

"I'll wait downstairs," he said as he headed for the door, giving the vanity and its now-cracked mirror a wide berth. Just before going out the door, he turned back. "Just be careful coming down those narrow steps."

"Will you catch me?"

Jack didn't answer. He just smiled again and left.

Jesus, girl, what's the matter with you? He finds you out cold on the floor and you start to flirt with him?"

In the bathroom, she splashed her face with water and quickly reapplied some subtle make-up. Surveying herself in the mirror she decided she wasn't too worse for the wear. No bruises, no bloodshot eyes. Still presentable. On the exterior, that is. Inside, she was a shambles. Hearing things, seeing things, passing out. It was all she could do to convince herself this was just the detritus of her breakdown tripping her up. Bound to stumble on it occasionally, Dr. Frankle had told her. The trick was to see it for what it was, to confront its irrationality. *Recognize the enemy in order to overcome it, right?* Without thinking, Kathryn reached for the bottle of Prolaxsis Frankle had given her, then pulled back as her better judgment intruded. Better to battle her nerves sober for the rest of the evening than to tempt fate, she decided. On the way out of the room, however, the sight of that cracked mirror almost made her reconsider.

She could see his shadow on the floor of the foyer as she came down the stairs. He was standing at the window, the very one where he watched his mother die all those years ago. She couldn't help wonder what that must have been like, living with the image of that. Even if he'd only been a baby, such a sight could never be forgotten. It must have nestled somewhere in the subconscious where it could fester. Who knew when it might surface, or what the effect would be?

He heard her coming into the room and turned. So gorgeous in his understated and classic grey suit and cerulean tie, which matched his lovely eyes. She didn't stumble, but his stare made her feel a little wobbly. It was the kind of frozen, slightly predatory stare men had when they wanted you.

"Hope I'm dressed properly," she said.

"Are you kidding? You make that dress look like a work of art."

"I hope you don't mind."

"Why would I?"

She chose not to pursue it. Either he knew this had been his mother's dress or he didn't. Either way, he didn't seem to care.

She made sure the front door was locked when they left.

THE NIGHT WAS CLEAR. The city glowed. They rode in silence as Miles Davis floated out of his Tesla's S1 sound system. Why spoil the elegance of the moment with mundane small talk, Kathryn convinced herself. Apparently Jack felt the same. He only smiled when he found her glancing at him. His car cruised so effortlessly down Wisconsin that she felt like they were gliding above the roadbed. But when they rounded the Naval Observatory and approached the British Embassy, her nerves started to tingle.

"You didn't tell me it was going to be *here*," she said.

"You were expecting the Elks Lodge?"

Valets swarmed the car as soon as Jack pulled up. Kathryn startled when her door suddenly sprung open on its own and a white-jacketed young man with impeccable manners and a BBC accent offered a gloved hand to help her out. As soon as she could without seeming desperate, she took Jack's arm, held on for dear life and tried to relocate some of the poise and confidence she used to shield herself with in situations like this.

An orchestra was playing somewhere in the distance. The crowd sparkled with Beltway movers and shakers, many of whom Kathryn recognized immediately. With the skill of one born to it, Jack easily navigated the warm acknowledgments and admiring glances. It seemed like everyone knew who he was, needed no introduction, was hungry for eye contact and recognition. They even deferred to Kathryn familiarly when he introduced her, as if she, too, belonged here by right. Probably just because she was with him, she admitted to herself, but she was relieved that if anyone had remembered Kathryn 1.0 they didn't show it, and she was pretty sure she didn't spot anyone from the days before her fall from grace. She allowed herself to feel comfortable, even attractive, making believe she was endowing the handsome, eligible Jack Wright with her presence.

"Is this how you usually spend your evenings?" she asked as he commandeered a tray of mini Beef Wellington hors d'oeuvres from a cute strawberry blonde server who was passing by.

"Occupational hazard," he chuckled. "Eat." He handed her three minis in a napkin while holding three more in reserve. "Then we can share some champagne."

"Hope you get combat pay," she said trying not to spill a

mouthful. "I've seen two Cabinet members, the Secretary of State and several congressmen already."

"And you're impressed?"

"Not my crowd," she said and almost added *not anymore, anyway* before she caught herself.

"It's easy once you learn the script," he laughed, "and don't improvise."

Kathryn felt a shudder sweep over her. She was swimming in his stare. Had he done homework on her? Did he know her history?

The band started a new tune. Couples were swaying on to the floor.

"Think you can manage?" Jack said as he put an arm gently around her waist.

"If you don't let go," she said as she took his hand. *Shit, there I go again!* But he swept her effortlessly into his arms and then to the center of the room. He was a great dancer and she quickly felt like they were inseparable, but she couldn't help noticing the furtive glances and curious whispers sent their way that were badly camouflaged with laughter and feigned indifference.

"It's funny, I never would have thought you were such an important businessman," she said.

"Why not?"

"I don't know. Your eyes. They don't seem ... hard enough."

"What would you have thought I was?"

"Maybe a teacher," she said. She didn't think that was right at all, but she felt the need to offer something.

"Not patient enough," he laughed.

"A doctor."

"Not smart enough."

She gave him a skeptical squint. "How about journalist?"

"Not cynical enough."

"Guess that leaves businessman."

"Why not lawyer?" he said, and she was sure he was holding her tighter.

"Not slippery enough," she said.

"How do you know?"

Her eyes met his and she was suddenly short of breath. He was definitely holding her tighter. It was not unpleasant, but Kathryn thought it felt slightly dangerous.

A man was making his way through the crowd toward them, indifferent to the couples who had to maneuver themselves out of his way. He seemed to float unnaturally through them, never once acknowledging their presence or recognition. He never blinked. His eyes remained riveted on her, and he had a slightly astonished expression as if seeing something extraordinary for the first time.

It was the same man from her hallucination! The one who had tried to kiss her before she passed out. There was nothing disfigured about the left side of his face, but this was definitely the same man. Older now, of course, mid-60s maybe, but still quite handsome and virile.

"This stunning creature is with you?" he said to Jack.

Kathryn felt suspended in time all of a sudden.

"I was wondering when you'd make an appearance," Jack replied. "Kathryn Fields, my uncle, Warren Wright. The man responsible for this wonderful charity event."

"So this is the young lady who bought Bob's townhouse." The man Jack called Uncle Warren took Kathryn's hand and kissed it. His lips were clammy. It was all she could do not to recoil.

"Be careful, Warren," Jack said. "She's a lawyer. Knows how to defend herself."

"I'm sure she does. But I'm too old to be politically correct. Jack tells me you're completely renovating the place."

Kathryn's throat felt dry and scratchy. "Little by little," she croaked.

"Finding walled up closets full of old clothes and forgotten trinkets."

"Jack told you, I see."

"Nothing important," Jack interjected, almost chagrined. "I sold all the best memories with the building."

"It's not that easy to dispose of memories, Jack," Warren said. He still hadn't taken his eyes off of Kathryn.

"You sound a little parched," Jack said to her. "I think we're ready for some champagne. Be careful of this politically incorrect old man. He will try to steal you away. And he's good at it."

"I'll be careful," Kathryn said as she watched him move away to a young man drifting across the floor with a tray of crystal flutes.

Without asking, Warren took hold of her and continued the dance. He was every bit as graceful and commanding as Jack. She was powerless to extricate herself.

"Darling, have we met before?" Warren asked as he held her firmly.

"I don't see how," she responded trying not to look at him.

"You look so very familiar. Such a lovely dress."

"Perhaps you're confusing me with someone else.," Kathryn said.

"I doubt there's anyone I could."

He seemed to drift away for a moment, and a kind of melancholy breached his poise. He was still looking at her, but his stare was middle distance, as if he was locating her in another time and space.

She held his stare with as much cool indifference as she could muster. And yet, and yet, something was stirring deep within her. Something mysterious and insistent. A taboo excitement she couldn't understand. Was it the fright of her hallucination suddenly come to life and standing in front of her? Or was it something more coercive and dangerous? Was she actually attracted to this man?

"You're trembling, darling. Are you okay?"

She realized he was right, and she was furious with herself. "I think I might be coming down with a bug or something," she said pulling away. "Don't want to spread it around."

"Cheers," Jack said returning with a glass for each of them. "So, has my uncle worked his magic on you yet?" he said touching Kathryn's champagne with his.

"I'm afraid she's immune," Warren answered for her with mock disappointment.

"I'm still feeling a bit woozy," Kathryn said taking Jack's arm. "Maybe I should make it an early night."

"Better do as she says, Jack," Warren laughed. "Or she might sue you for negligence."

"I'm sorry," she whispered to Jack.

"No, of course," Jack said. "Let's get you home. Warren can certainly handle the fundraising without me."

Kathryn summoned a smile. "It was nice meeting you," she said to Warren making sure not to add "again." He nodded in a way that made her believe he was thinking the same thing.

In the car, Jack kept the music so soft it could barely be heard. Was he giving her a chance to say something? She caught a glimpse of herself in the side-view mirror. Pale as cement, and just as cold.

"Want me to turn up the heat," Jack asked. Was she shivering that noticeably?

"Your uncle thinks we've met before." She left out the part about how she had encountered a younger version of him only hours before in her own townhouse.

Jack chuckled under his breath. "You'd remember if you had, believe me. Warren Wright is not a man who lets people forget him."

And that's what Kathryn was afraid of.

≈

WHEN THEY GOT to her townhouse, Jack escorted her to the door then stepped back to wait until she got the key in the lock and opened it.

"Next time, I promise not to punk out so early," she said turning back to him.

"So, there's a next time?"

The delight in his voice almost made Kathryn blush. "Sorry. Didn't mean to assume."

"Please, assume. It's very attractive on you," he said.

They stood there a moment. Was he going to try to kiss her? Would she let him?

"Go inside and make yourself a late-night snack. Then get some sleep. Tomorrow you'll be good as new." There was that smile again. He turned to leave, and suddenly she didn't want him to.

"Jack," she called out. "Thanks. I haven't been out on a date in a while. It was nice."

"More of a short story than a novel. But still," he laughed with a shrug.

She couldn't help laughing, too. She watched him get into his car and drive off, all the way down the street, until a stiff cold breeze swept over her and she realized she was trembling again.

She ignored Jack's admonition to make herself something to eat and went upstairs instead to chew on a Prolaxsis tab. This entire evening had spooked her. Especially her encounter with Warren Wright. She wanted the oblivion of sleep.

"What is wrong with you?" she muttered angrily as she shed the black dress and hung it again on the wall by the vanity with its cracked mirror, which she avoided looking at. How would she explain any of this to Dr. Frankle?

The cap of the Prolaxsis bottle impudently popped out of her hand and she had to grab a couple of pills before they slid down the sink drain. She dry swallowed one with a grimace, closed her eyes and hoped a wave of calm detachment would soon follow.

Instead, something moved in the mirror's reflection. Kathryn caught it out the corner of one eye. She spun around in time to see it come flying at her face. She threw up her hands defensively to bat it away, but whatever it was kept coming, grazing her face, getting tangled in her hair. Kathryn's hands flailed wildly until the thing freed itself and landed on the faucet. That gorgeous black butterfly, just sitting there fanning the air with its wings. The same one she saw earlier when she discovered the hidden closet. Had to be, it was so unique.

"It's okay, don't be scared," Kathryn told it. "You want to get out, don't you?" The butterfly responded by extending and retracting its wings. Kathryn moved slowly and deliberately to the bathroom window, hoping not to startle it.

"Look, it's a way out," she said as she gently opened the window. "C'mon, you can do it." But the butterfly didn't move. So Kathryn reached out a finger, sliding it slowly, unthreateningly, across the sink toward the little creature, which remained still even as she got closer and closer.

Finally, it stepped on to her fingertip and rested there. Kathryn raised her hand and studied it. Those scarlet markings on its wings glowed in the bathroom light. Step by patient step she moved over to the window and laid her hand on the sill.

"See, there you are. The whole sky is in front of you. Go on now, it's all right."

The butterfly made no effort to move off her finger, and Kathryn wondered how long she could stand here before she'd have to shake the thing off. Then, suddenly, the butterfly spread its wings and jumped. It circled the window several times before it finally veered away from the townhouse and disappeared. Kathryn slammed the window shut.

She stood there a moment staring out, then slowly sank down on the toilet seat and realized she was short of breath again. And she was shaking.

seven

Damn, she had great taste," Alex said, standing at the edge of that hidden closet holding Rebeca's little black dress up to herself. Though the mirror was cracked, she kept turning this way and that, admiring prisms of herself. She had dropped in to see Kathryn's progress on the townhouse, but the first thing Kathryn wanted to show her was the strange discovery in her bedroom.

"It was the oddest feeling, Al," Kathryn said from the foot of the bed where she remained, sipping iced tea. "Like a super-intense déjà vu." She was describing the peculiar sensation of meeting Jack Wright's uncle at the British Embassy. She deliberately omitted what had happened earlier, before Jack had found her passed out.

"How much wine you say you had?" Alex laughed.

"Just my mind playing tricks again, I guess."

Alex hung up the dress and turned to Kathryn. "Honey, there is nothing wrong with your mind. Get used to it, will you?"

"It's such a fascinating story, Al. A former supermodel, married into one of the city's richest families, murdered in cold blood on her anniversary. Her husband becomes a pitiful alcoholic recluse. Her son grows up without a mother."

"I never knew you were such a romantic."

"Her murder was never solved."

"Listen, hon, now is not the time to be grave-digging about some thirty-five-year-old unsolved."

"I'm not grave-digging. I'm just curious."

Alex shrugged and turned back to Rebeca's vanity. She couldn't resist picking up the Walther PPK pistol from that old memento box. "Sexy little stinger, isn't she?"

"What do you think I should do with it?"

"Keep it, of course. No self-respecting girl in this town should be without one." She noticed Kathryn frowning in one of the mirror shards and laughed. "Hey, I've got two." She put the gun down and caressed the dress again. "Tried it on yet?"

"Oh, I couldn't do that," Kathryn lied, then quickly wondered why.

"Afraid it's haunted?" Alex winked.

Kathryn startled. But not because of what Alex just said. "There's someone at the door."

And that's when the doorbell rang downstairs.

At the front door, Warren Wright was waiting. Dapper as ever. Kathryn was so dumbfounded by the sight of him that she just stood there mute. He seemed a bit disoriented himself. He had that bewildered squint that occurs when you see something you know can't possibly exist but there it is staring you in the face. Of course, he was too adroit to let the moment linger.

"May I come in," he smiled.

"Oh, of course. I didn't mean to be rude."

"Forgive the intrusion. I know I should have called, but that might have spoiled the surprise." He reached down beside the door to retrieve a stunning antique mirror. He carried it into the foyer with him. "I was having it refinished for my brother's wedding anniversary. Never got the chance to return it. Been collecting dust in my basement ever since."

Alexandra made no attempt to descend the stairs quietly. She wanted to be sure they heard her.

"Oh, Al," Kathryn said, grateful for the distraction. "This is Jack Wright's uncle. Warren Wright." And then to Wright, "Alexandra Gold, my best friend from college."

"And her guardian angel," Alex cautioned as she came forward to take Wright's hand.

"Yes, Brackenridge, Kelly and Levine. You handled some of my brother's estate, if memory serves." He let go of Alex's hand without waiting for a response and resumed his intense focus on Kathryn. "Anyway, after the other night I got to thinking maybe this might fit into your restoration plans."

"How very kind," Kathryn said, desperately trying to ignore Alex's widening eyes behind the man's head.

"It used to hang right here." He carried the mirror into the parlor, holding it up to the wall next to the fireplace. A low rumble rattled the windows. The glass trembled. Upstairs a closet door slammed shut.

"Damn trucks. Shouldn't be allowed in residential neighborhoods," Wright said as he leaned the mirror against the wall and stepped back to admire it.

Click click click.

It was the sound of a cigarette lighter in his pocket as he flicked the lid open and closed.

"I think the mirror would look wonderful there, Mr. Wright. I'm a little overwhelmed," she stammered.

"Don't be. What am I going to do with it anyway?" He took her hand and kissed it. "I'm happy someone is finally bringing this place back to life."

He turned to survey the room and appeared to drift off into another memory. "She had such style," he murmured so quietly Kathryn wondered if she'd really heard him. "Well, my driver's waiting." But just before he went out the door, he turned back. "It's Warren, please."

"You little stinker," Alex said after he'd closed the door. "Just exactly what kind of performance did you put on the other night?"

"What do you mean?"

"Honey, Mr. *Please, it's Warren* is one of the most powerful men in DC. Richer than God, better connected than Facebook. He was a boy-wonder in the Justice Department before he was thirty. Made a fortune with his brother before he was forty."

"I know who he is, Alex."

"Be careful, girl. That man doesn't take no for an answer."

A wave of nausea swept over Kathryn. She feigned a smile to keep Alex from noticing. "Chrissake, Al, he's old enough to be my father."

"There's a saying in this town, Kay. Power is the ultimate aphrodisiac. And, honey, that is one sexy guy."

The idea made Kathryn's mind ache.

GRAVE-DIGGING. That's what Alex called it. Excavating a tragedy that should remain past-tense, a dreadful footnote to a moment in time that ought to be allowed to rest in the peace of obscurity. Maybe she was right. What right did Kathryn have to be resurrecting it? What business was it of hers? After all, Andy Warhol was only partially right. In this era of *Breaking News*, even fifteen minutes of fame was starting to look piggish. Nowadays few things held people's attention beyond the next commercial interruption. Attention Deficit Disorder was endemic. There was always new dirt with which one could become titillated. New faces, new scandals. Meringue cookies that melted in the mouth so quickly nothing was left but a brief aftertaste of something cloying. If anyone remembered what happened to the gorgeous, wealthy and entitled Rebeca Wright thirty-five years ago, it would be fleeting and salacious at best. What purpose would be served by re-examining it except to upset those who had lived through it? Especially Jack.

But Kathryn felt compelled. The casual violence of Rebeca's death, the inconclusive investigation into the why of it, the tragic effect it had on her husband, let alone the indifference it bred in her own son, offended Kathryn. It was a crack in the wall, a stain on the carpet. Impossible to ignore. At least that's what she told herself as she ignored Alex's admonishment.

She stared at her office computer screen and a Vogue photo of Rebeca Wright and tried to imagine this beautiful young woman alive, vivacious and full of promise for a charmed and significant future among the influential and powerful. The kind of future for which Kathryn herself once seemed destined. Rebeca's mesmerizing stare was difficult to read, but it must have been the first thing that startled photographers in her early days as a much sought-after supermodel. Like the photograph Kathryn discovered hidden in that memento box, it didn't matter what the rest of her face was doing, smiling, pouting, flirting, seducing, or any of the other practiced poses a star like her had perfected. It was her indigo eyes that paralyzed you. They were deep wells. But of what, really? Curiosity? Arrogance? Diffidence? All of them at once? Was this a woman you could ever truly know?

It was almost noon and Kathryn realized she hadn't finished the case law summary Alexandra Gold had assigned her relevant to an appeal motion of Baltimore parents who were suing the Johns Hopkins Health System for the wrongful death of their infant daughter whose heart had stopped during surgery. Brackenridge, Kelly and Levine were representing Johns Hopkins, of course, and Alex wanted case law to support a defense that the corporation could withhold interviews conducted with several employees about the incident because they were privileged attorney-client encounters. But there was an ethical question here that troubled Kathryn, given the fact that it was Johns Hopkins attorneys who did the initial interviews then got the employees to agree to be represented by Hopkins counsel in upcoming litigation. BK&L was arguing there was no binding precedent to compel the hospital to turn over those interviews. Case law seemed contradictory and inconclusive. Kathryn's sympathies lay with the parents, but she knew Alex wouldn't be satisfied with that bias. So she quickly drafted a private memo to accompany her summary which argued that the best interests of all could be satisfied with a quick, quiet settlement accompanied by a non-disclosure agreement to keep the prying media at bay. A bit greasy, yes, but better than years of litigation during which the parents would be compelled to relive their daughter's tragic death over and over.

To her surprise Alex agreed with her assessment and was going to make the argument to her partners later that afternoon.

"Though I wonder if you would have been so squishy a few months ago," her friend clucked after reading Kathryn's memo. "You were always such an Amazon."

Kathryn wanted to defend her position as the most pragmatic, cold-blooded approach, but she conceded that "being on the other side of the looking glass changes one's perspective, I suppose."

And all she really cared about was getting back to that other side.

IT DIDN'T TAKE her long to track down where Roberto Gutierrez lived, and when he finally answered his phone he sounded almost relieved to have someone to talk to. He was one who remembered. He had discovered Rebeca. "I was a penniless fag photographer, a day away from starvation. She was a seventeen-year-old uncut diamond, working a food truck in Queens."

"Queens?" Kathryn asked. "Everything I've read said she came from an aristocratic family in Miami. A Brazilian diplomat father, an academic mother."

There was a small chuckle on the other end of the line. "I think maybe you'll want to come visit me so we can talk."

He lived in a modest but comfortable apartment in Baltimore's Highlandtown neighborhood, the decor tastefully coordinated and paired even if a bit threadbare. His photographs covered the walls, and Kathryn was not surprised that most of them were of Rebeca in her heyday. She had graced the covers of every major fashion magazine, been the face of numerous luxury goods, and it was almost exclusively Roberto Gutierrez who captured it.

"First of all, I was never her lover," the seventy-six-year-old Gutierrez said as he brought them tea. "Anyone who knew us realized how ridiculous the idea was, but it made good tabloid fare, so we encouraged it. Just another fiction in the myth of Rebeca Fedela."

"Fedela?" Kathryn asked mimicking Gutierrez' Spanish pronunciation.

"You're not writing a book, are you?" he glowered.

"God, no." She confessed that she had bought Robert and Rebeca Wright's townhouse in Georgetown and had become fascinated by her story, that's all. She left out the part where she'd met Jack, or had discovered Rebeca's dressing closet. And her gun.

He sat opposite and studied her a moment, possibly still deciding how much to trust her. Or maybe he was just uncomfortable admitting how much she reminded him of Rebeca. Finally, he sipped his tea and leaned back, eyelids drooping, his focus drifting as he nestled into his memories.

"We had a great run. By the time she was in her early twenties we'd had the cover of every magazine worth having," he said gesturing to the wall behind him. Her wary stare and androgynous physique were the perfect antithesis to All-American archetypes like Cheryl Tiegs, Christy Brinkley, or Cindy Crawford. And it was remarkably erotic. It ignited both men's and women's desires. "She was chased across continents by rock stars, politicians, royal pretenders, you name it," Gutierrez smiled. "Predators, all. She found it quite amusing, actually. We had an enviable life, and believe me, we took advantage of it. Jet-set gossip-drenched, paparazzi-pursued fame. Glorious. But I can assure you the enigmatic, multi-lingual persona Rebeca presented to the public was a far cry from the poverty-stricken background from which she'd emerged. All that business about a diplomat father and professorial mother was just well-curated bullshit," Gutierrez laughed. "Good copy for our PR people, but most importantly, it hid the stain of her background." Her mother had been a drug-addled prostitute, he told Kathryn. She never knew who her father was.

Rebeca was the most driven person he'd ever met, myopic about her career, militant about her market value, and fanatic about her independence. Her ambition never allowed her to indulge in any serious relationships. Love affairs were a distraction she refused to indulge. Such a fierce, aloof personality may have made her all the more intriguing, Gutierrez said, but her heart remained impenetrable.

"Until she met Robert Wright," Kathryn said.

"And his twin," Gutierrez answered with a frown.

"Twin? Warren?"

"Identical."

Kathryn tried to hide her shock by sipping tea and staring at the photos of Rebeca. "You didn't approve?" she finally said.

"Of Warren? No! But like most great athletes, Rebeca was smart enough to know that her career was destined to be short-lived. New girls were always on the horizon, and the fickle public was always ready for the next *thing*. She was tiring of the superficiality of it all anyway when he came along. He would pursue her to photo shoots all over the globe, drag her to celebrity social events, try to seduce her by every possible means."

"To be his trophy?"

"Oh, I never doubted the immensity of his passion," Gutierrez sighed ruefully. "But his kind of fire always burns too hot. It consumes everything in its path until the oxygen runs out, and then everything suffocates. Warren was a great high, but there was always a hangover."

"And his brother?" Kathryn asked.

Gutierrez's expression softened. "Robert was a gentle man, unlike his brother. He ultimately won Rebeca's heart with his kindness, his humor, his playfulness. Quite a prankster, that one. With Robert, Rebeca felt there could be comfort, consistency, a future. And never any hangover." Gutierrez chuckled. "Except after one of their fabulous masquerade parties. God, I miss those."

"Masquerades?"

"Oh, Robert loved them. An invitation to Robert and Rebeca Wright's on Halloween was a much-coveted ticket. Can you imagine? The great and powerful, camouflaged by elaborate masks. Remember, this was the eighties, after all. It's amazing no one has ever written a tell-all about what was said and done."

"And how did Warren take to being rejected?"

"What could he do?"

I wonder, Kathryn thought to herself. *That man doesn't take no for an answer,"* is what Alex said.

"Warren Wright was a businessman, above all," Gutierrez continued. "He and his brother had built an empire together. Nothing was going to jeopardize that. Nothing. Not even love, if that's what it was."

"What happened to you, then? To your relationship with her?" she asked tentatively.

A prolonged sigh escaped Gutierrez and his stare went blank. "We were as close as brother and sister. Until the day she died. She truly loved Robert. I know this. And I was happy for her. And even though it meant the end of our professional relationship, I came to respect Robert."

"But not Warren?"

It took a moment for Gutierrez to answer. "Warren Wright frightened me."

chapter
eight

For a brief while during college and law school, Kathryn 1.0 had used promiscuity to subdue the slow drip of embarrassment and guilt she could never quite turn off. She had convinced herself she didn't deserve love, but casual sex allowed her to own her desires. At least that's what she told herself. It was her choice. She was the one on the prowl, the one in control. And sometimes she let herself enjoy the whole messy, sweaty performance, wherever and whenever. But she soon learned an even more emotionally satisfying method of control, derived not from the promise of sex but from the denial of it. Her inaccessibility wasn't frigid or prudish, and she never used her elusiveness to tease, although truth be told, she couldn't help but enjoy the confusion of eager potential lovers who never understood why, even in this MeToo era of transactional timidity, this attractive, sensual woman couldn't be tempted. Somehow. And once she became the wunderkind of Watson, Cohen, Daniels and Marbury, she perfected the persona. To be unattainable was to be provocative, mysterious, powerful. She was Athena incarnate.

So the hormonal rush she felt at the sight of an exquisite and clearly expensive box of gardenias arriving at her office disturbed her. Her pulse accelerated, her skin grew hot. She couldn't help it, and she didn't like it. Was it excitement or trepidation? How was Kathryn 2.0 supposed to react? Of course she found Jack Wright attractive. Who knew where things might lead? But was she ready to find out? It had been a long time since she'd been with anyone. What if he was disappointed?

It took her a moment before she plucked the card from the box. As soon as she saw what it said, her hands began to tremble.

"Ooo la la." Alex's voice made her jump. "Flowers delivered to the office for everyone to see." She was standing in the doorway, a suggestive grin tugging at her lips. "Holding out on me, eh? C'mon, spill. Who's the lucky guy?"

"Oh, just a little thank you from Russell." *Good Kathryn. Nice recovery.*

"Russell? Is he hot?"

"My carpenter, Al."

Alex nodded suspiciously. "You must be paying him pretty well."

"Don't be vulgar."

Alex's laugh could be heard all the way down the corridor when she left.

Kathryn picked up the card again and studied the handwriting.

"*Some modest beauty to grace an office that already has it in abundance. Warren.*"

Warren. Warren Wright.

The scent of the gardenias suddenly made her nauseous. She tore the card into tiny pieces and stuffed them deep into her trash basket. And that's when the phone rang.

She glared at it. What if it was him, calling to find out if she was pleased with his gift of *modest beauty?*

"*Yes?*" she said with edge that was meant to deter.

"Wow, hard day?" Jack. Sounding like he was standing right next to her.

"Oh, Jack, sorry. Yeah, it's been a little stressful around here," she said as she closed the box of flowers and shoved them aside.

"Bet a nice meal and some good wine could calm the waters," he said, and she imagined that wonderful smile seeping through the phone line. "Besides, you owe me a do-over from the other night."

"Oh, I don't know if I'd be very good company, Jack. Rain check?"

"Sorry. Fresh out of 'em. I can swing by, say eight o'clock? I have a nice place in mind. Quiet, casual. Comfort food. Say yes. Please."

Her mouth moved before her brain had a chance to restrain it. "Guess I could use some comfort. Food that is."

He laughed easily and hung up.

Just like that, she thought. Another date.

THE PLACE JACK had in mind was indeed quiet and casual. Except for an older couple who hardly spoke to each other, they were the only two there. Greek food. Family owned. The owner knew Jack and set them up at a table near the back. They were never given menus. The food just started arriving. All of it very good.

"My father courted my mother here," Jack said as he speared olives and feta. "Kyros always made sure they had this table. Away from the windows so no one could see them. He asked her to marry him here."

"Very romantic," Kathryn said. An irresistible fantasy suddenly swept over her. She was the gorgeous and famous Rebeca Fedela being wooed over candlelight by the handsome and wealthy Robert Wright while greedy and frustrated paparazzi stood outside in the rain straining for a glance.

"I used to get him to bring me here," Jack continued interrupting her reverie. "Don't know why. It was never a pleasant evening."

"Maybe the memories were too painful." *Something I can identify with*, she thought.

"My father was the creative genius type. Barely out of college when he formulated a tricyclic compound called chlorprothixene. Marketed under the brand name Prolaxsis."

"I've heard of it."

"Wright Pharmaceuticals was founded on it. Made us a fortune." He sounded almost embarrassed.

"Glad to have contributed to the bottom line."

"Oooops," Jack said.

"That's okay," she said. Her smile diffused the tension. "In law school we used to call it "chillaxsis."" She chose not to say what she called it these days.

"Anyway, Dad lived in the rooms of his mind. And after my mother's death," he didn't say "murder," Kathryn noticed, "he retreated even further behind their doors. On my infrequent visits between boarding school and fancy summer camps, our conversations were what you might call labored."

"Sounds like a lonely childhood."

"I think I reminded him of her absence. But I never really knew her. Couldn't empathize. All I knew was that I didn't have a mother, and slowly but surely I was losing a father. To be honest, I was happier not being home." A naked melancholy had crept into his voice.

"That why you joined the Marines?"

There was a long pause as Jack bore into her with those dazzling eyes.

"Sorry," she said. "I couldn't help looking you up on Wikipedia."

"My declaration of independence," he smiled, echoing Kathryn's own remarks when she came to his gym.

"So how does a former Marine end up running a Fortune 500 company?"

"Helps to have an uncle who founded it."

"Must be a lot of pressure and responsibility."

"Want to know something? I could chuck it all tomorrow."

Kathryn raised an eyebrow. "C'mon … really?"

"Just set sail down the Chesapeake. See where the wind takes me."

"In a very luxurious boat, no doubt."

"Wanna come?"

Okay, Kathryn thought. *Might as well live dangerously.*

"What would Uncle Warren say?"

Jack didn't hesitate. "He'd be jealous."

That smile again.

And Kathryn's hot cheeks again.

"Sounds like a complicated relationship."

"Warren Wright became more of a father than my own ever was."

That sounded slightly defensive, Kathryn thought.

"My father died when I was very young," she said to shift the emotional ground. "My stepfather," she paused to gather her thoughts and make sure she didn't go too far, "he had a stroke three years ago and has been pretty much a vegetable ever since."

"I'm sorry."

"My mother isn't." And neither am I, Kathryn wanted to add. *Son of a bitch got what he deserved.* But she restrained herself. "I think she feels liberated. It wasn't a good marriage." *And I am the living proof of it.* "Wow, bet this isn't the lively conversation you had in mind when you asked me out, is it?"

Jack laughed. "So when's the furniture gonna arrive?" he said.

"Furniture?"

"You can't live in that place without furniture. It'll feel like a tomb."

The word "tomb" sent a shiver down her spine. "I don't know. Haven't decided what I want. Can't really afford too much at the moment." She left out the part where she refused her mother's persistent offers to decorate the townhouse.

Jack seemed pensive all of a sudden, mulling something over. Then he looked up at her like a kid with mischief in mind.

"Let's take a ride."

IN SOUTHEAST WASHINGTON, across the Anacostia River between RFK Stadium and the Navy Yards, there are several city blocks of concrete bunkers euphemistically known as public storage spaces. Monuments to our acquisitive culture, mausoleums for peoples' superfluous belongings, most of it destined for landfill eventually, or "Storage Wars." Jack's Tesla cruised silently through the canyons of hulking blockhouses with their retractable steel doors and heavy-duty padlocks until it arrived at one of the largest units at the far end of the complex. Kathryn waited in the front seat wondering what kind of date this was turning out to be while he unlocked and raised its clanging barricade. The Tesla's halogen headlights flooded into the space illuminating clusters of furniture, carefully covered and organized around a silver Mercedes 380SL convertible coupe.

Jack turned and waved for her to join him.

"I put everything in here after Dad died. Never got around to disposing of it."

Kathryn strolled among the chairs and tables, the rolled oriental rugs, the lamps. All high-end and bespoke. No Ikea or West Elm in here. But it was the Mercedes that called her name. Dusty but well-maintained, not a spot of rust anywhere. The chrome was shiny and smooth, no pitting or corrosion, the leather was still supple and buttery. Kathryn couldn't help caressing it with her fingertips.

"My mother's car," Jack said. "A wedding present from my dad. He just couldn't part with it. Go ahead. Sit in."

Kathryn met his eyes, which sparkled with encouragement. He

opened the door for her. She settled in and took hold of the steering wheel.

A jolt surged through her body that took her breath away. She felt like she was falling. She jerked away as if bitten by a pent-up charge of static electricity. Jack took no notice. He was coming around the car to get in the passenger seat. He dangled a key hanging from a gold chain. An enameled pendant was engraved with the letter "R."

"Go on."

She hesitated, then let impulse win out. She put the key in the ignition. The engine awoke with a well-tuned and powerful purr. Kathryn looked over at Jack wide-eyed. He nodded toward the door.

"Are you serious?" she said.

"Like I said, let's take a ride."

Within a few minutes, Kathryn and Jack were cruising along Suitland Parkway, top down, wind whipping at their hair, as she maintained a polite fifty-five miles per hour. Pat Metheny and Lyle Mays traded ethereal jazz licks on WJZW. With the woods on either side of the road, she could almost make believe she was meandering through the countryside in Virginia where she grew up.

"Don't be a wuss," he said. "There's no traffic. Give her a spank."

Kathryn glanced at him. He was clearly enjoying her enjoyment, so she nudged the accelerator. The Merc responded like a thoroughbred, surging effortlessly to sixty-five, then seventy, then seventy-five. She felt the momentum push her back into the seat and she heard Jack laugh. She eased through turns with a mere touch of the steering wheel. This was a precision instrument, and it seemed to Kathryn that the more it was challenged the better it responded.

On the radio, Matheny's group surrendered to another more

familiar melody. Chet Baker's version of "Autumn Leaves" started to harmonize with the wind. If Kathryn recognized the tune, she didn't show it, but another jolt suddenly surged across the steering wheel, fusing her hands there in a white-knuckle grip. Her pulse raced, her breathing accelerated with each additional MPH, her eyes widened and riveted themselves to the road ahead. She looked on the verge of sexual climax. Jack turned to see her lips part as if she were panting. Her eyes were watering from that unblinking stare. He glanced down at the speedometer. The Merc hit eighty.

"My get out of jail card expired last month, case you're interested," he said. She didn't answer, didn't look at him, but she eased off the gas ever so slightly and made a turn onto the Alabama Avenue exit ramp.

"Not sure we can get back on the parkway from here," he said, confused.

She ignored him, sprinted up the ramp to Alabama and made a left turn while hardly slowing down. They passed housing projects and rundown mini-malls, but there was little traffic and Kathryn seemed oblivious to stop signs and traffic lights.

"Might be a good idea to slow down now," Jack said, his voice even and undaunted. But after she blew through three solid yellows-turning-red, he decided enough was enough.

"Kathryn!" he commanded.

She either didn't see or didn't care about the stop sign in front of them and the three boys on electric scooters approaching from the right. Instead, she pressed hard on the gas pedal and sped into the intersection, barely missing the kids, who hopped off and dropped their scooters just in time.

"Kathryn, pull over," he shouted.

Her eyes suddenly blinked and her back stiffened. Her foot slid off the accelerator as if pushed by some unseen force, and the car drifted to a stop outside a stone guardhouse that stood at the gated entrance to a long drive along manicured grounds. Could have been an entrance to a country club except its snaking road eventually led to a complex of dark institutional-looking brick buildings that loomed in the distance on a hill like hulking beasts waiting to stampede.

"I'm sorry, Jack. I wasn't paying attention. I got lost in the moment." She looked astonished.

What she was afraid to tell him was that she couldn't even remember how they got here. Somewhere along Suitland Parkway she lost all sense of time and space. A grim fog had settled over everything obscuring the road. She felt paralyzed, although she could sense the steering wheel turning, the vehicle accelerating. She could hear Jack's voice, but it sounded so far away, and she couldn't understand what he said.

"You seemed to know where you were going," Jack said trying not to sound angry.

I had no idea, she wanted to say. *I wasn't driving!* "I didn't mean to upset you, Jack. I guess I just got carried away."

"Maybe I should drive us back."

She didn't argue. She slid over to the passenger seat as he came around the front of the car to take the wheel. But when he backed up to turn around, she caught sight of a tarnished brass plaque attached to the pillar of that guardhouse.

St. Elizabeth's Psychiatric Hospital.

Jack pulled up in front of Kathryn's townhouse and turned off the engine. They sat there a moment without talking.

"I'm sorry," she finally said without looking at him. "I guess I'm in the habit of spoiling nice evenings these days."

"You didn't spoil it. You just delayed my surprise, that's all."

"Your surprise?"

He took the key out of the ignition and handed it to her. "You can have it," he said as he wrapped her fingers around the fob. "As long as you promise to slow down."

"What?"

"The furniture, too. It's yours, if you want it. Take whatever would fit your decorating scheme. A lot of it is very fine. Unless you don't like any of it. And that's okay, too, although," he said with a wink, "I'm pretty sure you like the car. Right?"

"It's all very beautiful, but I can't afford stuff like that, Jack."

"You don't have to. I'm giving it to you. No strings. Please. You'll be doing me a favor, believe me. Consider it a house-warming present."

"But what about you? Won't you want it, some of it at least, sometime?"

"I'm a minimalist with a one-bedroom condominium at the Watergate. What am I going to do with it?"

"I don't know what to say."

"Say yes." And he didn't say 'please' this time.

She couldn't stop staring at him. How could she possibly accept something like this? She hardly knew the guy. Sure, he said *no strings*, but that usually meant *you'll find a way to thank me eventually.* And yet, he seemed so genuine.

"Let me think about it," she finally conceded.

"Of course. As long as you want. Stuff's not going anywhere." And he didn't seem at all disappointed.

"Thank you," she said, and she leaned over to kiss him on the mouth. His eyes widened with surprise, but he didn't recoil. She did. "I don't know why I did that."

"I don't care why," he smiled and leaned in to return the kiss with a gentle one of his own. This one lasted longer. His lips fitted perfectly over hers, soft and warm, confident and lingering. Not sloppy or aggressive. Just the right merger of passion and tenderness. Things began to escalate. Their breathing quickened, their hands started to roam, until he stopped and leaned back to caress her face with his fingertips.

They both looked surprised.

"So … what happens now?" she whispered.

"I'm not sure," he said as his eyes drifted all over her face.

"I haven't been with anyone in a long time, Jack." She was doing her best not to tremble.

He pulled her back into his arms and stroked her hair. "How 'bout a raincheck?" he said. Then he kissed the top of her head and started to get out of the car.

"Where are you going?"

He looked down at her and smiled. "After that little grand prix on the parkway, I could use a good walk. I'll catch an Uber when I tire out."

He walked off a few yards, then turned back. "Don't forget to lock it," he said. Before she could object, he was gone around the block.

Kathryn sat in the car a few more minutes, dazed by his generosity. By his kiss. By the bedeviling blackout she experienced while driving.

She got out of the car and hurried up the walk to her front door. Then she remembered, and quickly ran back to lock the Mercedes. What a beautiful automobile. She couldn't wait to drive it again.

Suddenly she felt someone watching her. But when she turned to look up at the bedroom window next door, Miss Dupree was not there.

Had she been there watching? How long?

For several days, Kathryn tried to ignore the slow churn of anxiety in her stomach. It would come on at the oddest times. In meetings at the firm while she was trying to concentrate on the case at hand, at home in the middle of the night when she got up to pee, on the Metro while she stared out the window at the beautiful fall leaves. There was no apparent catalyst, no predictable pattern. Just a sudden and dull dread that made her queasy, a faint but throbbing indigestion that her mother used to dismiss as 'nervous gut,' but that Annabelle, their housekeeper, used to say was a 'worriment.' She meant a premonition.

It hadn't come on this frequently since just before she went to Japan with her old boss, just before she'd lost her mind, drunkenly insulted the Prime Minister and ended up confined to the proverbial padded room. The time before that was, well, the time before that Kathryn refused to think about. But why now? Things were going so well. Why would the 'worriment' return now?

It was Jack. His fault. The movers had simply shown up, and before she knew it they were bringing in furnishings from his storage space, wondering where she wanted them. Why didn't she call Jack and ask him why he had presumed to know what her answer would be? Why didn't she tell the movers take it all back?

She knew why. She didn't want to. She made excuses for his audacity and presumption. In a perverse way they made him attractive to her. And though it seemed like a clichéd, some might even call predictable response to the inscrutable male, she couldn't help it. He was damaged. Vulnerable. No surprise given his family's notorious history. She recognized all the signs. Her mind said resist, but her nerve endings were too susceptible. To be honest, she feared the attraction a little, but she was also excited by it. So Jack was risky, perhaps even hazardous to her emotional equanimity, but there was a part of her that needed to prove she could handle it. Her recovery demanded it.

"You really don't want to put this in here, do you?"

Her mother was standing by the parlor entry with two of the movers who were straining under the weight of a massive oak coffee table that looked as if it had once been the door to some 18th-century Spanish mission. Sloane had "just happened to be passing by" after a Neiman Marcus shopping spree. A rather expensive excursion if the number of store bags she dropped in the parlor were any indication.

"This is where it's supposed to be," Kathryn said signaling the men where to deposit their burden. *Where it always was,* she thought but couldn't say why. She was standing by the fireplace, fixated on the Edith Piaf album cover, "Autumn Leaves." The title of the song Kathryn thought was coming from Miss Dupree's townhouse next door. But *Miss Dupree don't listen to no music. She's deaf.* Kathryn discovered it in a sleek Henredon credenza the movers delivered earlier along with a classic Harmon Kardon stereo system.

"It's so cumbersome," Sloane muttered, glaring at the coffee table. "Not really our style."

"What style is that, Mother? Pre or post Rex?" She put down the LP and finished winding the antique mantel clock that came with everything else. A gorgeous Westminster chime acknowledged the half hour.

Sloane ignored her daughter's shade about her stepfather and went back to the foyer.

"Here, fellows," Kathryn said, handing the movers a thin wad of twenty-dollar bills. "Divide this up among yourselves."

The men thanked her and headed out the front door to their van which was parked on the street next to the Mercedes Jack gave her. She turned back to the room and couldn't believe how perfect everything looked. It all fit. It all belonged. How crazy was that?

The "worriment" faded and Kathryn forgot all about it until she turned to see her mother in the foyer moving an English ladderback chair with a worn rush seat away from the door to a dark corner where it was hard to see.

"Better here, don't you think?" Sloane said with a self-satisfied smile.

~

"WE THINK Kathryn is making great strides," Dr. Tami Frankle said, clicking her ballpoint pen.

"Yes, *we* do," Kathryn said, sitting at one end of the couch opposite Frankle's chair. Her mother was sitting at the other end. Both had sour expressions. The distance between them was not quite three feet but it might as well have been the length of a football field.

"Great strides?" Sloane muttered. "Accepting a car, a household of furniture from a man she hardly knows?"

"I was doing him a favor."

"For what in return?"

"Oh, please."

Neither one looked at each other. They spoke directly to Dr. Frankle as if she were some kind of intermediary, some kind of magical interpreter that could convey words and intentions, thus avoiding the need for direct contact.

"Doesn't it seem strange," Sloane pressed on, "she wants to live in a house full of other people's belongings? Dead people at that."

"I offered to pay for it. Besides, it's all perfect for that house. Like it's meant to be there. Like I'm meant to have it."

"Seems positively ghoulish to me."

These family sessions are agonizing, Kathryn thought. *Why does Frankle insist on them? Every time I think I'm free, I'm yanked back into a cage.* "Why can't you just leave well-enough alone?"

"What makes you think you should be left alone?" Sloane hissed. "Moving up here by yourself, into that crypt of a townhouse. Rushing back to work. It's too much. Too sudden. You're still too fragile. And now you're dating all of a sudden."

"I am *not* dating."

"What do you call it, then?"

They still hadn't looked at each other.

"I'm losing her, aren't I?" Frankle stopped clicking, surprised to realize that Sloane was talking *to* her and not *through* her. "I'm losing the daughter I had."

"The daughter you wish you had," Kathryn smirked.

"And you're losing the only person who has always loved you." Sloane's voice quivered.

Kathryn rolled her eyes at her mother's typical 'stage-mother' melodrama. "You never loved me, Mother. You loved your idea of me."

"Are we going to start that again?"

Kathryn finally turned to her mother, and the fury in her stare made Sloane recoil. "Why don't you admit it, Mother? I was never going to be the perfect little Kate Hepburn clone you wanted. I could never be. And then I went and proved it, didn't I? So you sent me away."

"I ... thought it was best," Sloane mumbled, "at the time."

"It wasn't my fault!" Kathryn shouted.

Sloane groaned as if punched in the stomach.

Frankle put down her pen. "I think this would be a good time for a break."

It wasn't my fault! Kathryn repeated in her mind.

But then another voice chimed in.

"Of course it was."

SHE WAS LYING on her bed when the smell woke her up. The session with Dr. Frankle and her mother had exhausted her, and she must have fallen asleep while studying case notes for an upcoming meeting because it was already dark outside. She hadn't turned on the lights yet. The room was a dim blur of amorphous shapes and shadows. The smell, though, was distinct. And pervasive.

There was someone standing at the foot of her bed. Staring down at her. A silhouette. Vague and insubstantial. A man. Or maybe a woman with short hair. Hard to tell. Kathryn was momentarily paralyzed with shock, but the figure remained immobile, indifferent to the fact that she'd awakened to discover it there.

Kathryn grabbed for her beside light and turned it on. There was no one. Only a silky wisp fog hovering where the figure had been.

And still, that smell of smoke. Cigarettes. The one vice Kathryn never indulged because the very hint of it made her nauseous. More than one party was abandoned, more than one lover discarded, more than one piece of clothing washed and re-washed because she was too sensitive to the toxicity lingering in the air, on his lips, clinging to the fabric. Hotels and rental cars were a particular hazard. "No Smoking" warnings were often ignored, and no amount of cleaning or air freshening could completely erase the violation. So it didn't take much more than a whiff or two for her to realize that someone was smoking in her home.

THUMP!

Distinct and percussive. Outside her door. Something falling. Or someone moving something. Someone in the house. No doubt about it.

A shadow moved across the room. Kathryn spun toward it only to realize it was her own reflection in the mirror above Rebeca's vanity staring back wide-eyed and slightly crazed looking. She slipped off the bed and padded over to the vanity where she opened the jewelry box to retrieve Rebeca's pistol. At the bedroom door she could hear movement downstairs, and the smell of smoke in the hall was more acrid. She snuck out of her room to the top of the stairs and peered over the banister. The steps seemed to go on forever, vanishing into a deep well of murk.

But someone or something was definitely moving down there.

When she reached the foot of the stairs, she could see a shape gliding across the parlor. She stepped as quietly as she could to the edge of the pocket door protruding from the wall. She raised the gun.

Are you kidding? You don't even know how to use this fucking thing!

Maybe the sight of it would at least scare the intruder away.

Or prompt him to shoot back.

Kathryn put a hand on the pocket door and abruptly shoved it back. It hit the end of its track with a loud *BANG*.

The silhouette whipped around and screamed.

Which made Kathryn scream back.

"Kate, it's me!" Sloane's voice jumped several octaves. "It's Mother!"

Kathryn rushed to the wall and threw the light switch. Sloane was by the fireplace, ashen and shaking.

"Goddammit, Mother, you scared the shit out of me!"

"*Scared you?* I'm afraid I might have wet my pants."

"What the hell are you doing here?"

"I stayed in the city to have dinner with Tif and Buddy Montgomery. I told you. Remember?" Sloane was so breathless and parched she squeaked more than spoke. "I left my Neiman Marcus bags here."

"So how did you get in?"

"The door was unlocked."

"Unlocked?" No, that's not right, Kathryn thought.

"I suppose you think you can be lackadaisical about such things now that you've started playing with guns."

"I could have shot you," she shouted. *And I almost wish I had.* "Why didn't you call?"

"I didn't want to bother you."

"Bother me?" Kathryn started pacing the room. "You sneak into my home like some common thief. *You didn't want to bother me?"*

"I'm sorry, Kate. I didn't think you'd gotten home from work yet. The place was so dark."

"Were you just in my room?"

"What? No!"

"Smoking? Are you smoking again?"

"What are you talking about? I just wanted to get my shopping bags."

"And maybe do a little checking up on me while you were at it …"

"Of course not …"

"… maybe sneak a peek around the place …"

"I would never …"

"… see what kind of kinky shit your deranged daughter was into these days."

"Don't need to sneak around," Sloane said never taking her eyes of the gun in Kathryn's hand. "You're doing a good job of demonstrating all by yourself."

Kathryn realized she was waving the weapon around while she was pacing.

"Please, Kate, put that thing down, will you?" Sloane croaked.

Kathryn almost started laughing at her mother's distress. The whole situation was utterly absurd. Like a scene out of some turgid Cornell Woolrich melodrama. Here she was going all macho with a gun she didn't even know how to use, freaking her mother out. She went over to that *"cumbersome"* coffee table and put the gun down.

BLAAAAM!

It went off.

Sloane screamed hysterically and threw herself backward into the nearest chair, which almost flipped over. Kathryn just stared at the gun, too stunned to move.

The phone started ringing in the study across the hall.

"I think you better go now, Mother," Kathryn said in a flat, dispassionate tone of voice. There was no argument from Sloane. She grabbed her Neiman Marcus bags and fled.

Kathryn picked up the gun. There was a faint trace of graphite emanating from the barrel. *Jesus Christ, I didn't even know it was loaded.*

The phone continued to ring in the other room. Maybe one of her neighbors calling to complain. Maybe the police. She rushed to the study and picked up the receiver.

"Hello?"

There was no answer, just static and distortion.

"Hello? Who is this?"

A voice was barely audible in the noise.

" … it's not fair …" Sounding far away. "The way you make me … it's your fault…," the voice complained before it became subsumed in the static.

"Rex, is this you?" Kathryn gasped, fearing that her bed-ridden stepfather might actually have recovered enough strength to grab his bedside phone.

"… your fault …" the voice rasped again sounding like it was somewhere in the past.

"Look, I don't know what you want," Kathryn said, "but just so you know, whoever you are, I'm an attorney. And as soon as I find out who this is, I'm gonna sue your ass into the next century."

A squeal of feedback shrieked. She slammed down the phone. She was suddenly dizzy and had to grasp the edge of the table to keep from stumbling.

She wobbled back to the parlor to get the gun and put it away when she noticed her front door had been left slightly ajar after her mother fled. She pushed it closed and made sure the lock engaged.

She hadn't left it open when she got home. No matter what Sloane may have said, she had *not* left it unlocked. *So how did my mother get in?*

Kathryn noticed that Sloane, in her panic, had left one of her Neiman Marcus bags by the stereo. A drawer of the Henredon credenza there had been dislodged by the bullet and was sticking out. She went over to push it back, but the damage had ruined its track and it wouldn't go all the way. Kathryn pulled the drawer out to feel around. Maybe there was a chip of wood in the way. Or maybe the bullet itself. She swept her hand back and forth and fingered the hole to see if she could find it. Instead, her palm grazed something else, something stuck to the side of the drawer space with a piece of scotch tape. A torn piece of paper. No, not paper. A ragged piece of photograph. Of a strikingly handsome man in a tuxedo. With his arm reaching out across the tear.

Kathryn recognized instantly what it was. She took the torn photo upstairs to her bedroom and retrieved the other half from Rebeca's memento box. Sure enough, the pieces fit together. Rebeca standing between these carbon-copy men. But which one had received the humiliating banishment to the drawer downstairs?

Her husband, Robert?

Or his twin?

Warren Wright.

Kathryn was having a hard time concentrating. *Didn't get enough sleep last night,* she told herself. Or the night before that, for that matter. Too many strange dreams. Disturbing dreams most of which she couldn't remember. Only some disconnected fragments that soon decomposed. Wandering through the hallways of her family home in Virginia, or maybe not her home, similar but divergent in significant detail, a simulacrum she couldn't find her way out of. She thought she was following someone until she realized she was the one being followed. Someone was tracking her, someone she could never see but could feel, just around the corner, in the other room, at the top of the stairs, behind a closing door.

It had been like that every night this week.

Ever since she went down to the cellar.

She and Alex had left some boxes of books there to store until she got settled and could decide where they'd go. But the other night she'd finished the Anne Rivers Siddons book and needed a new diversion before lights out. The place was damp and dark and smelled like wet dog. From the top of the stairs her flashlight beam threw abstract shadows across the dirt floor below, and she wouldn't take another step until she located the light switch on the wall next to the door. A single bare bulb didn't dispel the gloom much but at least she could see that there were no boogeymen waiting to spring out of the shadows. The ceiling was low and cramped with thick beams holding up the floor above. The cold stone walls of the foundation were gray and jagged. This was where one realized how old the house was. *They just didn't make 'em like this anymore.*

Kathryn quickly found her book boxes and started pushing through titles looking for something that might simultaneously interest her and put her to sleep. Nothing appealed in the first one she opened, so she shoved it aside to search the next. And that's when she noticed the steamer trunk shoved haphazardly in a dark corner by the furnace. It was similar to one her mother used when she sent Kathryn away to boarding school. But this was not hers. This was much older. She didn't notice it before because it hadn't been there before, had it? But if that were true, how did it get here? Had the movers brought it from Jack's storage unit, put it here without telling her?

She shuffled over to the furnace and sat cross-legged on the floor in front of her discovery. There were no markings on the trunk, but it looked as if it might have come from a 19th schooner bringing immigrants from far away with whatever few posses- sions were most precious. The hinges were rusted iron loosely secured by rough and cracked leather straps, and they creaked bitterly when Kathryn raised the lid. It was filled with musty blankets and linens, some old clothes, Robert and Rebeca's presumably, and beneath them a frayed cardboard accordion file sealed in plastic and wrapped tightly with packing tape. Preserved against the elements, Kathryn thought. *Or nosy grave-diggers.* She was about to open it when she saw what was underneath.

A face. Staring up at her.

Kathryn jerked back and banged her head on a furnace duct. It was only half a face, actually, bisected from the left eye, across the cheekbone, through the upper lip and down the chin. It glared at her, this half face, this gaunt, sinister visage with its chalky complexion, hollow right eye and malevolent curl to what was left of the lips.

Kathryn poked at it as if it were a dead animal. Maybe diseased. Maybe not even dead. A strange sensation swept over her. A tickle of familiarity. But why? She'd never seen it before.

What was it doing here? What did it mean?

Kathryn could think of only one person who might know.

ROBERTO GUTIERREZ STARED at the mask on the coffee table in front of him, but he wouldn't pick it up. He didn't need to. He knew what it was.

"Halloween, 1982." he said. "Their last bacchanal. Legendary."

"You were there?"

"Of course, darling. I was invited to all of Rebeca's fetes. I told you, it was a prized ticket in this town. A perfect excuse to misbehave. I was always amazed at who showed up. Or to put it more precisely, who pretended *not* to be there. You weren't allowed to take off your costume or your mask. You had to be in character the whole evening. That was part of its perverse charm. It was rather liberating, to be honest. You wouldn't believe how much effort people put into creating their camouflage." He laughed at the memory of the famous and powerful hiding behind their false faces. "Can't get away with that anymore. Anonymity is a rare commodity these days. Like privacy. Used to be one could hide the deviance of one's desires. Not now."

"Some would argue that people who covet anonymity are often those who don't know who they really are. A convenient means of concealing an unsettled identity." *And I should know.*

"Oh, but haven't you heard, darling? A fluid identity is au courant these days."

So I am au courant, Kathryn shuddered. "Who did you go as?"

"Me?" Gutierrez laughed. "Myself, of course. I'm eccentric enough as it is, don't you think? Better looking back then, of course." His memories were clearly tinged with equal parts fondness and regret, Kathryn could tell. "I wore a suit that would make RuPaul pause, but by then there was really no need to pretend. No need of an alter-ego to take the blame."

"If you can't live out loud, what's the point, right?"

"We're all just characters, darling. Some in a story of our own creation, others in roles given to us. I prefer the former." He looked down at that awful face on the coffee table again with narrowing eyes. "I fear we may have overdone it that night, though."

"What happened?"

"Oh, nothing that outrageous, I thought. Just the usual intoxicated flirtations and sloppy conversation at first. There was some overheated wrestling around in closets, a rather nasty cocaine-inspired chest thumping between the Russian and French Ambassadors. Couldn't disguise their accents. We all knew who they were." Gutierrez laughed. "The usual boorishness. But things got a little strange near midnight. Don't know why. The atmosphere seemed to get heavier. At one point I saw a famous author, who shall remain nameless, threaten to rearrange his wife's face if she didn't stop calling him a horse's ass. The whole evening became slightly forced. The fun was strained. And Rebeca seemed off somehow. Distracted. I don't know. To me it seemed like she wanted to be anywhere but there. Everyone felt it. Maybe she was just bored with the whole thing. She kicked us out around one in the morning, which was early as those things went."

"What was her costume?"

"Nothing," Gutierrez smiled. "Nothing at all. Just a simple, gorgeous black dress." Kathryn felt her skin crawl. "After years of make-up, designer clothes and photo-shoot poses, I think she felt her own face was mask enough." He became quiet for a moment, and he mumbled to himself, "She was good at hiding things."

"And that was the last of their parties?"

"Never had another one. But then, she was pregnant. And Jack was born. No more time for frivolity, I suppose."

But there was something more, Kathryn surmised. Something more Gutierrez didn't want to talk about. It was the way he retreated from the conversation, sitting back, looking away, deliberately shrugging off the memory.

"So who wore that?" she prodded, nodding toward the half face on the coffee table. It took Gutierrez a moment to register her question.

"I really can't remember," he finally said.

He's lying, she thought.

Why would he lie?

WHAT MUST it have been like, she thought as she stood in the parlor listening to Edith Piaf's voice trembling out of the Harmon Kardon speakers with that dark lament of lost love and regret?

And those parties? What must they have been like? This home teeming with the most powerful and influential people in the city, liberated from their public personae by the masks they wore, freed to 'misbehave,' as Gutierrez put it. She stood up and turned to the mirror Warren Wright had given her and studied herself, impulsively pulling at her hair, lifting it off her shoulders and tightening it, framing her face in a helmet of fluff.

What if I cut it off? Cut it short. Like Rebeca's.

Kathryn 2.0 stared back from the mirror, fierce and adamant. Freed from the shame of her past, freed from an "unsettled identity."

"It wasn't my fault," she whispered and waited for the other voice in her mind to contradict her.

Instead, another sound caught her attention.

Click click click.

There, in the reflection behind her, was a dim figure, leaning casually on the door jam, watching her, cigarette in one hand, the other in a pants pocket, *click click click,* opening and closing a lighter. A slim, elegant figure in a tuxedo, its face veiled by the foyer's penumbra but not so blurred that Kathryn couldn't see what it was wearing. *That half face mask.*

She whipped around, but the figure was gone.

Or it had never been there.

She turned back to the mirror's reflection and thought she could see an oscillation in air where the figure had been. A slight shimmer in the shape of it, vibrating for a moment then dispersing.

And that's when Kathryn realized what she was wearing.

Rebeca's little black dress.

When did I put this on?

THE FIRST THING she noticed when she came downstairs in the morning was the mask. It was sitting on the ladderback chair. The one her mother had moved away from the spot Kathryn had chosen, orphaned to a dark corner of the parlor where no one would pay it much attention. It was back where Kathryn had wanted it. *Where it belonged.*

And the half face mask was sitting on it.

But I put it back in the trunk when I got home, didn't I?

She was still foggy with sleep. Shallow, restless sleep that even a couple of Prolaxsis tabs couldn't overcome. More bad dreams. More endless journeys through a house that seemed familiar until it didn't. Finding herself in front of a mirror wearing Rebeca's black dress. And someone watching. A man in a tuxedo. Wearing a mask. That awful grinning psychotic mask.

Maybe she had moved the chair after her mother left. *Could I have forgotten?*

She shook her head to dispel the cobwebs and went to the kitchen for coffee. And she noticed the credenza in the foyer was no longer in the front of the stairs where she'd told the movers to put it but on the wall leading to the kitchen instead. Lamps she had placed by easy chairs in the study had been switched, too. Even that cumbersome coffee table the movers struggled with in the parlor had been turned around. It was now facing the windows. All the furniture had been moved. The whole house had been rearranged.

And yet as Kathryn stood there stunned and disbelieving, the place looked right. Everything exactly where it should have been in the first place.

The only thing that hadn't moved was the mirror Warren Wright brought the other day. It hung exactly where he left it. Exactly where he said it used to be when Robert and Rebeca lived here.

chapter
eleven

Unwilling to submit to the "I'm-going-crazy-again" hypothesis, Kathryn decided to blame the meds Dr. Frankle had prescribed. After all, according FDA toxicology studies, which she spent an hour researching instead of doing her work, Prolaxsis was *"a potent antidepressant with potential alarming side effects that in rare cases persist even after use is discontinued."* There had been documented reports of users preparing meals, binging TV shows, even dangerous behavior like driving or operating power tools with no recollection of having done so.

How about rearranging a household of furniture?

But what would be worse, her inner voice challenged? Stop taking it and risk another psychotic episode?

"What's up with you?" Alex asked from the door to Kathryn's office, interrupting the internal debate. Kathryn jerked and knocked over her coffee cup, spilling its beige contents all over the desk.

"Shit! Always the butterfingers." A lame excuse which didn't convince Alex one bit.

"You okay? You've been a little distracted lately. Am I shoving too much work at you?"

"No, no. Not at all," Kathryn objected, wiping up the spill with soggy Kleenex tissues. "Bring it on." She thought of insisting more vehemently but decided that might be protesting too much thus confirming Alex's suspicions. But of course she did have too much work. What lawyer in a firm like this didn't? She couldn't let anyone think that, though. Not about her. Not now. Not with this new job, this new lease on life. She couldn't let anyone believe she wasn't up to it. She couldn't show any weakness.

Still, she couldn't get that half face mask out of her mind. Or the furniture that had been moved. *By whom?*

"Maybe your love life is getting too complicated," Alex winked suggestively.

"I wish," Kathryn smiled hoping to preempt her friend's obvious fishing expedition about Jack Wright or, God forbid, Uncle Warren.

"Well then, since you're such a glutton for punishment, c'mon."

"Where are we going?" Kathryn asked as she followed Alex into the maze of BK&L corridors.

"I'm putting together outside counsel to assist an important client's in-house. Class-action lawsuit. Gonna take years. A Permian Basin of billables, baby."

"Why me?"

"Well for one thing you're gonna be the smartest cookie in the room. For another," that mischievous smile pulled at Alex's lips, "you were requested."

When they entered the twentieth floor conference room reserved for the meeting, Kathryn couldn't catch her breath. Sitting at the far end head of the table was "Uncle" Warren Wright himself. He was flanked on one side by an assortment of her colleagues from BK&L and a contingent of other lawyers on the other side facing them, presumably Wright Pharmaceutical's in-house. There were bottles of still water, carafes of coffee and tea in abundance. A sideboard had been dressed with various breakfast pastries and fruit, but no one had availed themselves of the treats. No one wanted go first. So no one went at all.

Wright stood up when Alex and Kathryn entered, and everyone else followed suit.

"Gentlemen, ladies," Alex said, confidently taking a seat at the other head of the table, signaling Kathryn to sit at her right hand. "Since this a preliminary meeting, Chairman Wright and I suggest we simply introduce ourselves to each other this morning, and then everyone familiarize yourself with the briefs we've supplied so we can dive in seriously at our next meeting. Warren?"

Everyone sat down and picked through the folders of motions, opinions and precedents that Josh, Alex's factotum, had placed at each chair. Warren Wright remained standing, dominating the room with his stature, his charisma, his piercing stare, which swept the room like a drone camera looking for its target. It finally settled on Kathryn, and she knew it. But she wouldn't look back. Her inner Athena had emerged. She remained focused on her briefing book even though the words on the page might as well have been alien hieroglyphics.

"Someone once asked what the difference was between a good female lawyer and a pit bull," Wright finally said. There were nervous, stifled chuckles around the room. "The answer? Lipstick."

Was it politically correct to approve with laughter? No one could decide, so no one took the chance. Except Alex. She decided it sure enough was and enthusiastically embraced the joke.

"I put on my best shade for you, darlin'," she laughed. "We're gonna kick some ass."

"Exactly what I wanted to hear from BK&L," Wright laughed back. "These class-action suits are based on stunningly over-broad legal theories. Just a ruse to try this issue in the court of public opinion instead of the justice system. Unfortunately, since the attacks on Purdue Pharma for its opioid business have gained traction, it's turned into open season on all the rest of us. So let's be clear from the start, we have never misled the public or the medical community about the efficacy or the associated risks of our products. That said, we have no control over any medication's use after it is sold to distributors, pharmacies, after it's prescribed by physicians and enters the market. But here we are. So, at a fifteen hundred bucks an hour, I expect you all to come up with strategies to 'kick some ass,' as the intrepid Ms. Gold has promised, and drive these nuisance suits back into obscurity where they belong."

More nervous chuckling around the table as Wright finished his pontification and sat down. Alex then took the room.

Kathryn could barely hear what her friend was saying as she led the introductions and doled out assignments. The blood rushing past her ears was humming like leaf blower on max. She could feel Warren Wright's stare penetrating her clothes. He wasn't listening to Alex either. She couldn't wait to get out of that room. When Alex adjourned the meeting, she was the first one to the door.

"You've got to get me out of this one, Al. I'm not up for it," Kathryn frantically typed on her keyboard.

Alex pinged her right back. "Sorry, K, no can do. This is coming down from on high. When a client like Warren Wright asks, we bend the knee."

"Where are the flowers?" Warren Wright said leaning against the doorframe of her office with the nonchalant posture of the supremely self-assured. Kathryn looked up from her computer screen with a jerk. His smile was both friendly and arrogant, as if he knew the effect that it had and was not afraid to use it.

"Oh, thank you, it was very thoughtful of you, I took them home," she stuttered, glancing down at her trash basket hoping there were no tell-tale petals to give her lie away.

"I'm glad. I didn't want it to seem inappropriate. Hard to know these days." He was clearly fishing.

Kathryn managed an enigmatic smile. Neither to confirm nor deny. Let him wonder.

"Jack told me about the furniture," he said.

"It was such a generous thing to do. I didn't know what to say."

"You said yes. As you should have. It made for a beautiful home once." His eyes lost focus. Just like they had the night she met him at the British Embassy. "It was so exciting back then. Everything was fresh and," he paused until he found the right word, "… unsullied." He shook his head gently as if mourning the irretrievable passion of youth. "Some moments in time, you wish they could last forever."

Please leave, she thought. *Please, just leave.*

Wright straightened up as if he'd heard her. "I'm glad you're on our team. Your 'guardian angel' can't say enough about your skills."

"She exaggerates."

"I'm looking forward to finding out for myself." His smile had become abstract, and Kathryn couldn't decide what it meant. "Perhaps you'll invite me over to see how everything looks."

Kathryn's stomach clenched. That complicated taboo excitement was churning. She wanted to look away, but didn't want to give him the win.

"She loved gardenias," he said so softly that Kathryn wasn't sure she'd heard him correctly.

But then he was gone.

And she started to breathe again.

chapter
twelve

Kathryn's reaction to Warren Wright's visit in her office, *calculated to rattle her, no doubt,* was so confusing that she couldn't concentrate on the rest of the day's work. *What was it about him that made her feel so adrift?*

She ducked out of an impromptu post-work "mixer" of the Wright Pharmaceutical team after only a few minutes. It was just a pep rally anyway for the young associates to congratulate themselves on being chosen for such a prestigious assignment, beer and wine compliments of BK&L's partners, and Kathryn couldn't cope with the competition disguised as camaraderie. She wanted space. So she took off in the Mercedes Jack gave her for a drive through Rock Creek Park to clear her mind.

Her mind cleared, all right, completely in fact, leaving only a void of time about which she could recall nothing. And now, an hour later, perhaps longer, here she was, parked on in front of her townhouse, the car still running, with no recollection of how she got there.

In the side-view mirror, she caught a glimpse of a dark sedan parked down the street with a vague silhouette behind the wheel smoking a cigarette. *Staring at her?* Kathryn turned to get a better look. The man was gone now, but the driver's door was open.

All of a sudden, there was a loud bang and the Mercedes rocked on its wheels. She whipped back in time to see a man crushed against the passenger window, eyes rolled back, dropping to the street unconscious. For a split second Kathryn thought she recognized him. She jumped out of the car to help but realized that a gauzy mist had permeated the atmosphere. She was moving in the jerky half-speed of a dream. She shut her eyes and pressed her palms against her temples. *"Oh God, don't let me be losing my mind again."* When she finally looked up, hoping the scene had changed and that reality had been restored, a child cried out from her townhouse parlor window. A baby boy, calling to her. And in that split second someone grabbed her from behind and yanked her hair back. The glint of a steel blade flashed in front of her face.

"Are you all right, dear?" A hand on Kathryn's shoulder hit like a taser. It was Ms. Dupree out for her evening constitutional with Maggie the housekeeper. "We saw you standing there, swaying back and forth," the old woman said with her exaggerated deaf-compensating pronunciation and signing at the same time. "We were afraid you were sick."

"Oh no," Kathryn answered, feigning a self-deprecating chuckle. *I was just hallucinating about getting my throat slit.* "I was just thinking about the night she died. Rebeca. No one understands what really happened. It's such a mystery."

"Some things aren't meant to be understood," Maggie said caustically. "That's why they're called mysteries."

Ms. Dupree moved in closer to Kathryn and her voice became more intimate, her signing more delicate. "Just because you hear voices, dear, doesn't mean you're crazy. I hear 'em all the time. I'm deaf, but I'm not crazy."

Her stare made Kathryn feel like the old woman was looking through her. She turned away and stared up at the window where the child had been calling to her. "She must have been so scared," she said to herself.

Ms. Dupree leaned even closer and whispered, "She had a gun, you know. I saw her with it." She pointed to Kathryn's bedroom window. "She should have used it."

∾

WHAT WAS it about Rebeca Wright that so preoccupied Kathryn? Why did she continue to fixate on this woman and what happened all those years ago? Was her obsession causing these hallucinations? Or were the hallucinations the cause of her obsession? The question was a Mobius strip. No beginning. No end. A snake eating its own tail. The more you knew, the more you knew what you didn't.

And what about the furniture? Moved. Rearranged. That was no hallucination. How could she explain it? To whom would she even try? Alex? Jack? *I can't even explain it to myself, for Chrissakes.*

Dr. Frankle? Oh, hell no. Not unless she wanted to become reacquainted with the confines of GWU Psych.

She was sitting in bed holding the accordion file she'd found in that basement steamer trunk. She debated whether to open it, but conscience ultimately yielded to compulsion and she prepared to invade Rebeca's privacy. She carefully unwrapped the tape and plastic so she could put it back the way she found it. Inside were bundles of papers, old bills, insurance policies, scrapbooks with articles about Rebeca's career, photos and contact sheets taken by Roberto Gutierrez. There was an elegant calligraphed invitation on delicate parchment to Robert and Rebeca's wedding with her revision notes scribbled all over. *"Don't like this color. What about date? Add 'no gifts, please.'"* Another invitation had a cheekier tone. *"October 31st. 8 PM until the bell tolls. Don't you dare come as you are."*

And then she came upon a lengthy memo from an attorney named Collins. *No wonder this was sealed and hidden,* Kathryn quickly realized. Rebeca had hired him to locate and, if possible, identify her father, if he were still alive. Collins had tracked down several men who fit the profile Rebeca provided and the dates that would have corresponded to a timeline of her mother's pregnancy and Rebeca's birth, but he ultimately determined that there wasn't enough evidence to conclusively identify any of these men, two of whom were deceased by then, as Rebeca's biological father. This, of course, was in the days before DNA analysis was available.

In other pockets of the file was a collection of police arrest reports of a woman variously identified as Carmen Favela, Louisa Smith, or Irene Fedela. The name Fedela jumped off the page. It was Rebeca's true maiden name, according to Gutierrez. Carmen/Louisa/Irene had been incarcerated several times in New York and then in Miami for "solicitation." At various times, she was homeless and destitute, but "out of the life" for a number of years because she was "too old to attract much business." At the time of Collins' memo, she was working as a maid for the Catholic Dioceses in Queens, struggling to be drug free. There was a photo sandwiched among these documents. A middle-aged woman hugging an infant.

"THAT'S LOUISA," Roberto Gutierrez said when Kathryn told him about the photo she'd found. She had called under pretense of offering him the photos and contact sheets she'd discovered in the basement. "She was little Jack's nanny." He sounded drunk.

"The nanny?" She chose not mention the arrest reports the lawyer had left behind in his notes. "What happened to her? Is she still alive?"

"Who knows?" Gutierrez muttered. "They took her away after Rebeca died. Took her away." He stopped abruptly and she thought she heard him curse, as if maybe he'd said something he shouldn't have.

"They? Who? Took her away where?" She could hear his breathing accelerate on the other end of the line. It took him a moment to answer.

"Saint E's."

Kathryn's stomach flipped at the mention of the name. Saint Elizabeth's. The building she'd unwittingly driven to the night Jack gave her the Mercedes.

MORE AND MORE, Kathryn was feeling at the mercy of forces beyond her control. Some invisible hand was tugging at her, pointing her at things, compelling her to search in shadows, to investigate darkness, to seek answers to questions she hadn't asked. Because if she didn't, she'd have to admit she was coming undone. Again. And the thought of that terrified her more than what she might discover. If her obsession with what happened to Rebeca Wright was nothing but a psychotic mania triggered by old newspaper accounts, or the cryptic comments of a former photographer, a batty next-door neighbor or a private detective, if her attraction to Jack and his Uncle Warren was nothing but the by-product of that mania, then hope was lost. She should just commit herself and be done with it. Standing in the lobby of St. Elizabeth's hospital encouraged such dire thinking.

The past century and a half had not been kind to this place. Even in sunny daylight it was a brooding and ominous pile in serious disrepair on a bluff overlooking the Potomac and Anacostia Rivers. Opened in 1855, it was created to *"to provide care for the indigent and mentally ill of the District of Columbia as well as for the insane of the US Army and Navy."* The infamous and anonymous had been incarcerated here: James Garfield's assassin, Charles Guiteau, before his execution, John Hinkley for thirty-five years after he shot Ronald Reagan, the poet Ezra Pound who spent over a decade often confined to the "hell hole," a building without windows where "patients" wandered without supervision, screaming and frothing at the mouth. Unmarked graves and the incinerator on site begged more than a few questions about what else may have happened to many of the poor souls who ended up here. Now, in the early evening twilight, the place simply looked impoverished and contaminated.

It took every ounce of Kathryn's courage to walk through the door in the first place, and every bit of her willpower to subdue memories of her own convalescence at GWU Psych. She had left after work and followed the same route as the night Jack's Mercedes brought her here. She didn't much drive here as let the car deliver her. It took the best of her bullshit about representing the Wright family and then some subsequent hushed conversation among St. E's staff before a supervisor acquiesced and allowed her to spend *"a few supervised minutes"* with Louisa.

The old woman was sitting in a dingy common room staring at Jeopardy on an eighty-inch Sony 4K TV. Apparently St. E's justified this electronic extravagance for its sedative utility. The other patients sitting nearby were certainly mesmerized. Louisa's hair was a tangle of straw. Her complexion was bleached and her eyes were watery and vacant. She looked hopelessly bored.

"Hi, Louisa," Kathryn said pulling up a chair. "I'm Kathryn."

When Louisa finally looked up, her eyes blinked rapidly and a tiny smile desperately tried to emerge. Kathryn thought she saw a spark of recognition sweep over the woman's face, but it vanished as quickly as it appeared, like the flare of a match. Indifference and ennui returned.

"I know who you are. You bought the house. They told me."

"Yes, I did. It's lovely. I'm very happy there." *Was she? Was that what she meant to say? Or was it just a reflexive response to keep the conversation going?*

Louisa bore into Kathryn with her eyes. "Have you met her yet?"

"Who, Louisa?"

"My daughter."

There it was. One of the answers Kathryn had been seeking. "Rebeca?" she said. "She was your daughter?"

"No! I was the nanny," Louisa barked, dismissively contradicting herself. "They were good to me. I loved them. Robert was so good to her. And that darling boy." She drifted away into herself.

"He's all grown up now, Louisa. Very handsome."

"He never comes to see me no more."

"I found a picture. Maybe you'd like to have it." She pulled out the photo she'd found in that basement trunk. The one of a younger Louisa holding the baby Kathryn now knew was Jack Wright, her grandson. She offered it to Louisa who glanced at it but wouldn't take it. Kathryn shifted her chair a little closer, sneaking a furtive glance with peripheral vision at the nurse who was keeping a discreet but watchful eye a few yards away.

"I think Rebeca is trying to tell me something, Louisa," Kathryn said softly. This got the woman's attention. She looked up at Kathryn now with a steady and clear-eyed stare. "I think she wants me to know what happened back then. You were there that night. Can you tell me? Can you tell me what happened to Rebeca?"

"He killed her," the old woman said as her face twisted with pain.

"Who? Who killed her? Do you know?"

"And then he took me away from Jack. Never should have done that."

Be careful, Kathryn told herself. This woman is breakable. One wrong word might set off a manic episode. *God knows I've seen that happen before.* She gently took Louisa's hands in hers and massaged them tenderly. She felt the nurse stiffen slightly in her chair. "That must have made you very sad," she murmured to Louisa, "to have to leave like that, to have to leave the little boy you loved so much." The nurse relaxed when she saw Louisa smile.

"He was so beautiful. Just like his mother," Louisa said. She squeezed Kathryn's hands. "You look like her."

"You said *he* took you away from Jack. You mean his father? Did he send you away?" She pulled another photo from her pocket and laid it on Louisa's lap. It was the photo she found in Rebeca's memento box now taped together with the torn piece she discovered in the parlor credenza. A perfect fit. There was Rebeca, standing between her husband and brother-in-law. How similar the two men looked. Even their expressions. But on closer inspection, a marked difference was apparent. It was the set of the eyes, the curl of the smile. There was something genuine and inviting about the man to Rebeca's left. Robert, her husband. It was the way Gutierrez described him. There was something frigid and calculating about the twin on the right. Warren. Had to be. His eyes weren't looking at you, they were evaluating you. The same way he stared at Kathryn the night she met him at the British Embassy. And now Rebeca's expression made more sense. At first, Kathryn had thought she was staring straight into the camera, but in this conjoined photo it was obvious she was looking slightly to her right, at Warren, with his abstract smile. Instead of wariness, the expression on Rebeca's face now seemed to Kathryn to border on acute hostility.

Louisa withdrew her hands from Kathryn's and picked up the photo.

"Was it Robert, Louisa? Did Jack's father send you away after Rebeca died?"

A tear escaped Louisa's eye, and her hands started to shake.

"I'm sorry, Louisa. I didn't mean to upset you." Kathryn reached for the photo, but Louisa wouldn't give it back. "Let's talk about something else," Kathryn implored, trying to pull the photo away. Louisa yanked it back. "Louisa, what is it? What's the matter?"

The old woman lurched for the tray of supper sitting untouched next to her. She grabbed a plastic spoon from the plate and broke it in half. Before Kathryn could stop her, she began to stab the photo, mutilating it.

"Louisa, stop. What's wrong?"

The woman was keening like an animal in its death throes. The nurse was on her feet, rushing to them, grabbing for Louisa's hands.

"What did you do to her?" she bellowed at Kathryn.

"Nothing. I don't know. I showed her a picture…"

The nurse ignored her. "Louisa, give me the spoon, dear, everything's all right. Let me have the picture. Give me the spoon. It's all right."

But it wasn't all right. Louisa was out of control. She slashed at the nurse with the broken spoon, opening an ugly gash on the woman's cheek. The nurse howled in pain as Kathryn jerked away in horror. The other patients in the room were finally roused from their stupors and were chiming in with laughter and screeches of their own. Two orderlies suddenly appeared to restrain Louisa. The photo of Rebeca, Robert and Warren floated to the floor in the struggle where splatters of the nurse's blood smeared the image.

"You better leave," the nurse snarled through the bloody fingers clutching her face.

Kathryn grabbed the photo and ran from the room with the catcalls of other patients chasing her down the halls. She made several wrong turns and suddenly found herself lost in a corridor of resident rooms that smelled of bleach and musk. Several patients wandering in bathrobes and nightclothes turned to see her standing there. Some seemed amused by her confusion and desperation. Perhaps they knew the feeling all too well.

"Welcome back, darlin'," an unshaven man said, leering at her from the doorway to his room while he rubbed his crotch.

Kathryn bolted back the way she came. Eventually she found some exit doors and burst through them into the parking lot. When she got to the Mercedes she dropped her keys and had to crawl on hands and knees under the driver's door to retrieve them. That bloody photograph was on the ground next to them.

Kathryn picked it up and glared at it. The photo was punctured and bloodstained. It was as if Louisa had been trying to cut out the heart of the man to Rebeca's right. Warren Wright.

Kathryn fumbled again getting the keys into the ignition but eventually got the car started. Just before she pulled out, she was sure she heard laughter coming from somewhere close.

Kathryn was sitting in front of the Watergate, that infamous collection of buildings next to the Kennedy Center, trying to decide if she should go through with it. The encounter with Louisa at Saint Elizabeth's had rocked her world. She didn't know how to process it. She needed to talk to Jack about it even though she feared what his reaction might be. He wasn't too thrilled when she brought him the mementos from Rebeca's keepsake box. How would he feel about her tracking down the nanny who was with him the night his mother was murdered? How would he react to the photo she'd found hidden in his parents' furniture, a picture that drove his former nanny into a frenzied act of violence?

An intimidating security guard, big as an NFL lineman, in a black suit that barely concealed the bulge of his gun, had been dispatched to find out what she was up to. She was about to put the car into reverse when Jack appeared in the lobby and saw her. After a quick brief by the security guard, he came outside.

"Are you all right?" he said as he leaned in uncomfortably close through her window.

"I was driving home," she said, "thinking about some things, and … I know I should have called, but do you have a moment?

You think we could go somewhere and talk?" She suddenly realized she hadn't considered the possibility he might have 'company' upstairs. Maybe he'd make up some lame excuse about the hour or work he had to do. Instead, he smiled that charming smile and actually seemed pleased to see her.

"Sure. You could come inside." When she didn't answer right away, he offered, "Or maybe we should go someplace neutral, if that'd be more appropriate?"

She looked up at the notorious building where once a president's paranoia had brought about his downfall.

"I've heard it was haunted," she said trying to sound casual.

"Yeah, there have been rumors about guys in plumbers' overalls sneaking around late at night trying to finish the job," he joked.

He makes it so easy, she thought.

He signaled the wary guard, who pushed some buttons on the security console opening the gate to the garage.

A few moments later, Jack led her into his condo.

A simple one-bedroom was what Jack called it when they first went out together. The description was woefully inadequate. It may have had only one bedroom, but the space was palatial. On the 14th floor with exquisite views up and down the Potomac. True to his word, Jack was indeed a minimalist. The furniture, what there was of it, was sleek and functional. There was little personality, but everything felt expensive and unique. Even the kitchenware seemed designer-inspired, and the appliances weren't just modern, they were futuristic, with IoT-enabled sensors that *dinged* intermittently like annoying assistants pleading to be helpful. Pale and subdued lighting came on or went off when one moved from area to area. Kathryn noticed several Amazon Echo Dots lying in wait around the apartment anticipating being summoned to service. But there were hardly any personal items in view. No photos, no objéts. The art was abstract and impersonal.

And the place was clean. Ultra clean. Either this man was fastidious to a fault, or he had an army of staff who swept through the place on an hourly basis, paged by Echo no doubt, if a speck of dust floated within electronic range. The impression it all made on Kathryn was that of a five-star hotel suite. Or the kind of home one could walk away from at a moment's notice.

"I hear you're joining our class-action litigation team," Jack said as he went to the kitchen to pour some wine.

"It was your uncle's idea, apparently." She noticed a shadow pass over Jack's expression, but it vanished as quickly as it arrived and he smiled as he brought her the wine.

"My uncle knows talent when he sees it," he said.

"I'm feeling a bit awkward about the whole thing."

"Why on earth should you?"

Because I'm being haunted by your mother and the house I've bought? Because I just met the woman who might be your grandmother? In the pocket of her slacks, she fingered the photograph that Louisa stabbed. *Or maybe because I'm going crazy again!*

She let go of the photo and pulled her hand out.

"I just don't want to let anyone down," she averred, chickening out. "You both have been so generous, and now this new assignment at the firm, I'm beginning to feel a little like a moon in planet Wright's orbit."

"I understand. We have a habit of …" He searched for the polite way to put it.

"Not taking no for an answer," she said filling in the blank.

He nodded a bit sheepishly.

"Please, don't misunderstand," she qualified. "I'm not ungrateful. After the year I've had, it does the old ego good to find validation wherever I can."

"You don't need validation, Kathryn."

God, he'd be so easy to fall in love with, she thought. But the other voice in her head mocked the very idea. *But what would Uncle*

Warren say? "You might not think so if you knew the truth of it," Kathryn mumbled.

"Want to talk about it?" he said so non-judgmentally he might as well have been asking what she'd had for lunch. For some reason she decided that he wouldn't be critical, that he would listen patiently, try to understand, try to be a friend instead of a fucking therapist.

She started tentatively, a bit evasively, trying to read him, maybe change course if she sensed discomfort or censure in his expression. After a sip of wine she began, "My friends and I used to play this game when I was a kid. 'What's the worst thing that could ever happen to you?' I always won."

"What was it, your worst thing?"

"Being buried alive."

Jack laughed. "Yeah, that'd be pretty bad."

"Screaming for someone to hear you ... but knowing they never will. You can't move, can't tell day from night. You're alone in the darkness. And you'll be like that, in the dark, forever."

He didn't take his eyes off her, but unlike Dr. Frankle with her annoying pen-clicking and bated stare, she could tell he wasn't calculating a response, wasn't pondering a way to lower her deeper into the trauma well so he could *'get at the root of the problem.'* Instead, he looked like a little boy listening to a story, wanting to know *what happens next.*

"When I got older, of course, being buried alive became more of a metaphor."

"For what?"

"The emotional sarcophagus I was withdrawing into. The dark loneliness that was closing in on me. Like some metaphysical shrink-wrap."

"What brought it on?"

Something I did. But you don't know me well enough to hear about that. "I think maybe I was always susceptible. I just needed some catalyst to tempt me." *And I was ready to be tempted.* "I just didn't recognize what I was doing at first. Then when I did, I tried all kinds of strategies to break out of it. Sex, drugs, rock 'n roll. Those didn't work, of course. So I tried ambition. I thought I could beat it back with success. That seemed to work."

She got quiet for a moment, and Jack filled in the silence. "Until it didn't," he said.

Okay, so here's the finale, Jack. "I had a nervous breakdown last year." She waited for his expression to change, and it eventually did. From intense curiosity to what she could only interpret as empathy. It threw her off-balance, but *in for a dime, in for a dollar.* "They called it a psychotic break. Brought on by severe, undiagnosed depression and anxiety, overwork, and exacerbated by a narcissistic social justice warrior complex and the liberal use of alcohol."

Jack's eyes smiled. "Yep. That'll do it every time."

"Basically, I made a fool of myself and embarrassed my boss in front of the Japanese Prime Minister and the press. They shipped me home where I continued to behave like a royal ass until everyone got fed up and threw me in jail. I ended up with a six-month staycation at George Washington Psych."

She expected him to try the encouragement strategy, telling her he couldn't believe her behavior was that bad, telling her she was doing just fine now, reminding her that but for the grace of God we all could be just one bad day away from mental ruin, that the bad weather was sure to change if she was patient. Instead, he nodded and sipped his wine.

"You think it helped?" he asked. "The staycation? Get you back on your feet?"

"If I'm honest, yeah, I guess. I couldn't go on the way I was. Too many demons tormenting me. I had to confront them. Or at least learn how to quiet their voices." She took another polite sip of wine. This would not be the time to get sloppy and confessional. "I learned one big thing, though."

"What's that?"

"Maybe being buried alive wouldn't be any worse than never getting out of GW Psych. Now that would be hell."

"What was it like?" Again, that guileless curiosity.

"It wasn't the Snake Pit, if that's what you're thinking."

"Jesus, I hope we've progressed a ways from that."

"In some ways it's a little more insidious because it's so well-intentioned. The drugs, the therapy. Unless you're an irredeemable socio-psychopath, they really do want you to get better and leave. The loss of privacy, though, physically and emotionally, that's the bill that must be paid. The notion that one could have secrets was anathema. If you had secrets, you couldn't be helped. If you held things back, because they were precious to you or because you were ashamed of them, that was prohibited. No matter how you tried, they were clever enough to ferret them out. They were really good at chipping away who you were. Sooner or later, you were stripped of any mysteries you used to construct and protect your identity. There was nowhere to hide. And that was necessary, they felt, because then you could be rebuilt, purged of all your corrupt data, or the sneaky viruses that were plaguing you, so that the reboot was clean."

"Sounds a little like Marine bootcamp."

They were quiet for a moment, both lost in the privacy of their experiences, which no amount of talking could bridge. It was a comfortable quiet because neither one expected the other to probe. In that moment, they understood each other, and any tension that might have been goaded by such a conversation, simply wasn't there. It surprised Kathryn.

Now was the moment. If she was going to confess her hallucinations or hauntings or whatever they were, if she was going to tell him about Louisa and the photo that set her off, now was the time.

"I'm afraid, Jack."

"Of what?"

"I don't want the darkness to come back."

Jack put his wine down and took Kathryn's from her. Then he pulled her into his arms and laid her head on his chest. It was such a calm and confident thing to do that she didn't resist. He just held her, gently stroking her hair. His breathing was slow and calm. He was not aroused. But when she looked up at him, he kissed her. It was too chaste for her, so she encouraged him by pulling him closer and banished her inner Athena. That was all the permission he needed.

He was a tender lover. Slow and considerate, willing to search for ways to turn her on before indulging himself. Everywhere he touched her, everywhere he kissed was unpredictable and really effective. If she hadn't been so eager, she might have thought it too studied, too practiced. But she was grateful he was that good. It allowed her to be unrestrained without feeling self-conscious. By the time she could tell he was ready to lose himself, he'd already brought her to the brink. They both came together, hard and long.

❧

"Darling ..."

The voice was soft and seductive. The murmur of it caressed the back of her neck. But it wasn't Jack. She came awake abruptly from the best night's sleep she'd had in weeks, no dreams, just blessed oblivion, to find that he was already up and gone. There was a note on his pillow.

"Good morning, darling. I'm sorry I'm not here to see you wake up. Duty calls. But I watched you sleep all night, and I'll be thinking about that all day. J."

A slight morning-after regret began to creep over her. She lay there and tried not to question her behavior, but the inevitable gut-check kept intruding on her thoughts. Yes, it had been a long time since she'd been with anyone. Hormones were easily stirred. She was vulnerable. He was charming. The stars were aligned.

Who could blame a girl for indulging herself? But had there been something else? Had she subconsciously deployed a defense mechanism against the perils of a Warren Wright? A pre-emptive shot across her emotional bow? Using Jack to shield herself from her simultaneous fear of and attraction to the older man? One could get lost in this kind internal debate. And her body was feeling too good. Her feelings for Jack weren't contrived, dammit. The physical expression of them last night only reinforced their intensity.

She slipped out of bed and went to his closet for something to put on. She wasn't ready to erase his scent with a shower and her own day-old clothes. She'd relax into the morning. Have some coffee, show up late for work unconcerned about her endorphin glow. Predictably, his clothes were neatly arrayed by color and style. Like the rest of his apartment, everything in its place. She was reluctant to take anything too fresh and pressed, so she grabbed the shirt he'd left on the chair by the bed and held it to her face. He was present in every wrinkle and fold. The moment she put it on any doubt she felt about her motives last night was dispelled.

His Jura coffee maker was tricky to operate, but the espresso it finally produced jolted her into a hyper alert state. She hadn't felt this clear and precise in a long time, and she recalled the self-assuredness she used to have on mornings like this, the fearlessness that had propelled her early career.

The egocentrism that sabotaged it, too, her other voice reminded her before she shut it down.

She went over to the desk by the windows to leave Jack a note of her own. She had intended to tell him what happened at St. E's last night before passion intruded. Maybe this way would be easier anyway.

Sure, her inner imp suggested. *That way you don't have to face his reaction. If he's really pissed about you snooping around in his family history, you'll just never hear from him again.* But this was about his mother and what happened to her after all, she answered back. Why wouldn't he want to know?

His desk was pristine. Of course it was. Not a thing on it except for an Apple Retina 5K monitor, a Logitech wireless keyboard set to the side as if hardly ever used, and two or three manila file folders neatly stacked next to it. She sat down by the windows and stared out at the glistening Potomac while she composed her thoughts.

"Darling Jack..."

She opened a drawer to search for some paper and a pen.

And that's when she saw her name.

It peeked out from the bottom of some papers that had been shoved toward the back. A shiver of embarrassment swept over her, as if she'd just stumbled into Mommy and Daddy's bedroom while they were fucking. She pulled out the file and placed it on the desk in front of her without opening it. What could possibly be in it? And what was Jack doing with it?

She finally worked up the courage to look.

And instantly regretted it.

It was a private investigator's report. Detailed with credit checks, criminal background research, employment, banking and property data. And most damning of all, a timeline narrative for the incident in Japan, her arrest back in the States and subsequent confinement to GW Psych.

He knew all along. The bastard knew about the breakdown all along.

Kathryn stared at the report and all the accompanying documentation the PI had acquired including police reports and mug shots of her incarceration after Japan, records that were supposed to have been sealed and expunged. And yet, here they were, accompanied by the PI's explicit summaries of conversations with various authorities and eye-witnesses.

So this is what Jack's money can buy!

Kathryn dropped the file as if it were radioactive. Her heart was pounding and she thought she might faint. She felt violated, betrayed. She didn't know whether to scream or cry. *How could he have pretended not to know?*

A dark rage began to grow inside her but the fury quickly morphed into cold contempt. So, he was just another rich and privileged son of a bitch who assumed he was entitled to know whatever he wanted about whomever he wanted and had the power to pursue it without permission or fear of consequence.

She found a Sharpie marker at the back of the desk drawer. With bold, violent strokes across the top of the file, she finished the note she had wanted to write, different now, but just as heartfelt.

"Darling Jack...FUCK YOU!"

aybe she should have given him a chance to explain. After all, there was nothing in the file she found in his desk that wasn't true. She had, indeed, done everything documented there. Still, what right did he have to intrude into her life like that? Was it something he would use against her in the future, something he'd use to manipulate her? No matter how much she tried to rationalize it, she couldn't reconcile his behavior with the man she thought she knew. Or *wanted* to know.

He called several times and left messages on her voice mail because she wouldn't answer the phone. Each time, he was apologetic and remorseful. It was a mistake, he said. The work of an overzealous investigator. Part of a background check he did before selling the house.

He did a background check on someone wanting to buy a house?

Kathryn should understand, Jack persisted. His uncle, his company, their public profile, they had to be very careful about any transactions they were involved in.

Bastard. Your sense of entitlement is disgusting.

No one else had seen it, Jack pleaded. In fact, he hardly looked at it himself.

Sure, you didn't. Probably got you off, didn't it Jack? Fucking a psycho like me? Something strange and different, maybe a good laugh to share with your boxing buddies about how crazy I was in the sack?

Kathryn finally stopped listening to Jack's messages after she realized she was talking back to them.

She felt the shrink-wrap tightening.

She didn't leave her house for the next two days. She slept a lot. Didn't eat much. Time was of no consequence. Day drifted into night, then back into day. She made a few calls to the office to get updates from colleagues on the Wright Pharmaceutical case and offer apologies for the 'stomach flu' that had felled her, but for the most part she sat in the parlor staring at the walls, or lay in her bed staring at the ceiling or at Rebeca's small vanity across the room.

She finally beat back the gloom to make one trip out of the house. To the offices of Dr. Tami Frankle at George Washington Psychiatric Hospital. The regularly scheduled appointment with her "parole officer." It would be more problematic to miss it, Kathryn reasoned, than to brave the outside world. She didn't intend to bring up the report she found in Jack's apartment. Hell, she didn't intend to bring up Jack at all. She just hoped she could get through Frankle's probing and pen-clicking without resorting to profanity, which would provoke Frankle into more probing questions and Kathryn into more convoluted evasions.

"What made you do it?" Frankle asked after the perfunctory prologue of innocent sounding but calculated greetings. *"How have you been feeling/how's work/how's the new home?"*

"Do what?" Kathryn mumbled as she was caught momentarily off-guard by the non sequitur inquiry.

"The Prime Minister. What do you really think made you go off on him the way you did?"

So we're back to that, Kathryn thought. *Wasn't expecting this angle of attack.*

"I think it's worth re-examining, don't you?" Frankle smiled.

"I've told you. It was the dismissive and condescending tone he took when I brought up the subject of Korean comfort women. That and the copious amount of alcohol I'd consumed on an empty stomach after two hours of sleep." She was lying and became afraid Frankle would recognize it.

"But you'd been in many similar situations with difficult men before. Probably sensing the same condescension, the same dismissiveness. Right? No doubt you had many opportunities to lash out, but you didn't. You held back. You were a political animal, Kathryn. You knew how to play the game. Even with your inhibitions compromised by lack of sleep and copious amounts of alcohol, as you put it, I have to think there was something different about this time. What do you think that might have been, the proverbial straw that broke the camel's back?"

Click, click, click.

His smell, Kathryn wanted to say. The man's odor. That sultry amalgam of vinegar, rose water and grilled meat. It sent her over the edge. He must have never bathed, just layered himself with cloaking aromas. Mixed with some active perspiration and you could imagine a wafting breeze of rotting food, or the funk of wanton sex, depending on your predilections.

It was the smell of her stepfather.

"We've tried to analyze this before, you know," Kathryn said, trying to seem genuinely weary and frustrated. "*I've* really tried. Thought long and hard about it. But in the end, I think he simply rubbed me the wrong way. Wrong place, right time. Really had nothing to do with the comfort women. I just used them to pick a fight, and I'm ashamed of it. You're right. I've had to deal with a lot of guys like that. I guess I was just fed up. And he was the one in the line of fire. I fucked up. Pulled the trigger. End of story."

Frankle watched her with an unblinking stare, waiting, no doubt, for that slight 'tell' which would betray Kathryn's evasions and give her Torquemada all the evidence she needed to keep probing. But Kathryn maintained the penitent pose and muddled through the rest of the session with superficial insights and mean-ingless conclusions.

And without stumbling into any confession about Jack.

THE SEX that night reminded her of a boyfriend she'd had briefly in college. He would come home from a night out with his friends, slightly drunk and plenty horny, and though she was already asleep he'd try to rouse her. Which was not difficult to do. This was during her promiscuous phase where she enjoyed sex as often as possible. He would slide into bed and press his erection against her lower back, then slip a hand under her nightshirt to caress a nipple. All very gentle and teasing. He didn't speak, didn't try to roll her over, he just pressed himself tighter and tighter against her, kissing her neck, breathing faster and heavier into her ear while stroking her pubis. She skipped wakefulness and slipped from unconsciousness into mesmerized lust without any interme-diate awareness and instantly became so wet she almost didn't feel him enter her. He did all the work as she simply lay there eventu-ally drifting into a warm bath of orgasm.

She felt that way now. Not fully awake, but aware she was slowly being coaxed toward a full body spasm that would plunge her into a vortex of ecstatic oblivion. She could feel herself being thrust into the mattress. She arched her back and raised her hips, not to resist but to give greater access. Accelerating gasps skimmed across her ears. She felt a dozen pair of hands fondling her.

And suddenly the smell overwhelmed her. The acrid aroma of sulfur and vinegar. Her eyes flew open in time to see, or think she saw, a vanishing shadow rising up, groaning with pleasure. Its physique was amorphous and evanescent, and it was gone before she could scrutinize it, leaving behind only that lingering mordant odor. Kathryn jerked up, fully alert now and bathed in sweat. Her own face, flushed and wide-eyed, stared back from Rebeca's vanity mirror across the room. Had she been having a proverbial wet dream? Had she been masturbating in her sleep? Maybe that night with Jack had really stirred up the old hormones and taken over her subconscious.

She threw off the covers and stumbled into the bathroom. Her legs were rubbery, her loins were sore. She filled the sink with cold water and dunked her head into it up to her neck until she could feel the rosacea withdrawing from her cheeks. When she couldn't hold her breath any longer, she stood up and stared at her dripping expression as if pondering a stranger. Had she taken some of those damn meds earlier? She couldn't remember.

What she did remember was that smell, that bitter body odor.

chapter
fifteen

The next morning Kathryn almost chickened out several times and exited I95 before she reached Route 17 and the drive to Sugar Hill, her family's farm on the Rappahannock River near Fredericksburg. It had been over two years since she'd come anywhere close. Her infrequent visits with her mother took place at fashionable restaurants or The Cottages as it was simply known to Sloane and her set, the exclusive Bobby Jones-designed country club with its patrician membership and rarefied prejudices. But it wasn't her mother she came to see. She needed to confront a curse from her past. She'd been picking at the scab for a long time. Last night's fever dream made her think she needed to rip it off, but the closer she got the more she began to question whether this visit would be cathartic or simply drive her deeper into the confusion of her own shadows. As she turned on to the private road leading to the main house, she wondered if it was worth the risk. She'd stopped taking her Prolaxsis and was slightly regretting it now. Too late. She'd have to do this without any chemical defenses.

The pastures were still gloriously green, and Kathryn recognized several of the mares that were grazing there. The smell of fresh cut grass, of tightly bound hay bales, mixing with the fragrance of the Encore azaleas planted everywhere transported her momentarily to an early childhood, when everything seemed all graceful and balanced. Before the messiness of real life intruded.

Before her father killed himself.

And her mother remarried.

At the house, servants greeted her warmly. She'd spent more time with them than all the private school "friends" Sloane was continually urging her to collect, and no matter what had happened, they never turned their backs on her. The house was beautifully decorated with fall cornucopia, plaid throws, center-pieces of pears and apples, and lots of dried flowers. If Better Homes & Gardens just happened to show up for a photo spread, Sloane Fields was prepared to show off. Only one of the bedrooms upstairs would be off-limits. It was where Kathryn's stepfather lay barely alive in a hospital bed, hooked up to various medical devices, attended to by twenty-four-hour nursing care hired to interpret the dwindling needs of this near-vegetable.

Kathryn's mother had married Rex Baudry shortly after her first husband, William, Kathryn's beloved biological father, committed suicide when he lost all his money. Billy Fields had been a very successful bond trader in Richmond until ... he wasn't. Typical story. Speculative investments fueled by over-weening self-confidence and leveraged collateral couldn't survive the dotcom bubble burst at the turn of the century. His profes-sional demise was a scandal ready-made for Virginia society gossip. He couldn't take the shame. One evening after several martinis at The Cottages, he came home and used his prized Abbiatico & Salvinelli triple-barrel Excalibur 20 gauge to get the hell out of Dodge. Permanently. Kathryn was devastated, but her mother refused to cave. Discovering the unexpected, rather desti-tute circumstances she suddenly found herself in, Sloane Fields picked herself up and went on the hunt. Reginald "Rex" Baudry was the perfect prey, or so she thought. He was handsome, well bred, and rich. The problem, Sloane soon discovered, was that Rex was a slacker. He had inherited money and didn't need to work. That was all well and good, as far as Sloane was concerned, but since he had no need to exert himself, no ambition to be useful, Rex Baudry had plenty of time to indulge in whatever pleasure pursuits caught his eye.

And one of the things that caught his eye almost immediately was Sloane's daughter, Katherine. This was before she changed the spelling of her name in the aftermath of what came next. Rex set about conquering the sixteen-year-old beauty.

In reality, it was she who conquered him.

When Sloane found out, she had to make a choice. Kick Rex out, perhaps even take him to court, and return to the deprived circumstances husband number one had gifted her with his suicide, *or* send her daughter away to boarding school, bury the entire affair in a deep dark corner of her memory and continue to enjoy a lifestyle to which she'd become incurably addicted. Rex was only too happy to accommodate, provided she didn't interfere with any of his other pursuits.

Sloane chose Door Number Two and made peace with the terrible bargain she had struck. Her relationship with her daughter, now Kathryn, never recovered, but she comforted herself by feeding a self-serving narrative that her daughter's success in school and then later in her career could be attributed to her severe banishment and the subsequent isolation and loneliness that surely toughened her up.

Until the incident in Japan, of course.

Eventually, Rex Baudry was served a generous helping of his own deferred justice. After a night of heavy drinking and poker during a Kentucky expedition to mate his prized mare with a recent Derby winner, he had a massive hemorrhagic stroke that left him paralyzed and helpless. Which suited Sloane just fine. With Rex's fortune still intact, Sloane was able to bring him home and hire round-the-clock care, thus freeing her to enjoy his money without restraint. Rex never recovered from the paralysis of the stroke, although he had been known to mutter a few words occasionally, which, doctors assured Sloane, indicated he was fully aware of what had happened to him. There was no doubt that Rex Baudry was tortured by his condition and his inability to do anything about it. Sloane appreciated the irony of fate's vengeance. As for Kathryn, satisfaction was poisoned by guilt. *"Son of a bitch got what he deserved"* became permanently entangled in an inconclusive wrestling match with *"It was my fault."*

As she climbed the grand staircase, she avoided looking toward the room where she grew up and the lure of its memories, good, bad, and ugly. She hurried down a hall into what was once a servants' wing but now housed the vegetative shell of Rex Baudry. The room smelled like one in any hospital, a bit antiseptic, a bit medicinal, more than a bit fecal. The nurse sitting by the window reading a book looked up warily when Kathryn came in.

"I'm Sloane's daughter," she declared. "Just paying a quick visit." She went straight to the bed without asking permission. She hadn't seen Rex since she came to the hospital in the aftermath of his stroke. That was almost three years ago. He had been unconscious then, unlikely to survive, and her mother didn't want her there anyway. So she left the next morning and rarely spoke of him since. Her desire not to think of him met with less success. He was her burden, the reminder of her own selfish motives and agenda.

He stared up at her with his slack, immobile expression, but Kathryn knew by the frail squint of his watery eyes that he recognized her. The nurse watched vigilantly from across the room as the two of them communed in silent recrimination. Did he blame her for his condition, Kathryn wondered? Did she still stir a perverse lust somewhere deep within that impotent body of his, the kind of craving she used to manipulate so easily and effectively? Did he hate her for it? She hated herself for it, that's for sure. She was revolted by him still, but even more by herself, by her calculated rationalization that her Lolita impulse had been a deliberate strategy to take control of a situation she understood all too well. *And by the fact that she enjoyed it!* Yes, he was the predator and she was the prey, but she had turned the tables.

And look where it got them both.

Rex's open jaw began to twist back and forth as if he were trying to say something. The nurse was getting nervous. "Please, I think you're disturbing him," she said.

"How can you tell?" Kathryn asked sardonically, but she wasn't joking. She was genuinely curious to know if this wretched corpse could communicate. She wanted to know what he was thinking.

"Well, this is an unexpected surprise." Sloane's voice sounded almost hopeful as she stood in the doorway. "You could have at least let me know you were coming."

Kathryn turned calmly. "You left one of your 'Needless Markup' bags at my house the other night. I wanted to return it. I was told you were at the club when I called."

"Then why didn't you come there?"

Kathryn didn't bother to answer. Her reason was obvious enough. It was lying on the bed behind her.

By now the nurse was on her feet, sensing the sudden tension in the room. "I'm sorry, Ms. Fields, I didn't know this would upset him."

"It doesn't matter." Sloane said shifting her gaze to Rex. There was no mistaking the indifference, even the contempt in her stare. "I don't expect Kathryn intends to stay long, do you, dear?"

She sounds almost disappointed, Kathryn caught herself thinking. "The bag is in my car." She managed a serviceable smile and followed her mother out the door, but not before turning back to her stepfather. For a split second she thought she recognized an expression on that feeble, stroke-stiffened face.

Begging.

"The place looks nice, Mother," Kathryn said as they came down the grand staircase.

"You sound surprised."

"No, I'm sure it always looks this turned out."

"You'd know if you ever came to visit."

"You don't really want me to, though, do you?"

Sloane paused at the foot of the stairs and turned back. "No, I suppose neutral territory is always preferable." She held her daughter's stare a little too long. It was a look of disapproval mixed with deep sadness that made Kathryn very uncomfortable.

"Not much improvement, is there?" she asked with a nod upstairs toward Rex's room.

"There never will be, I'm afraid."

Don't you mean, "I hope"? Kathryn wanted to say.

Sloane smiled as if she'd read her daughter's mind. "Well, since you're here, I suppose we could have some iced tea out on the porch. You could tell me how you are, how things are at the firm." And when Kathryn hesitated, "You might find this hard to believe, but there are times when I really do miss you. We were friends once, I think."

For the first time, Kathryn saw something in her mother's eyes she couldn't remember ever seeing before. Loneliness.

"I have a conference call scheduled end of day," Kathryn lied. "Need to get back."

Sloane nodded, but her stare couldn't help narrowing. After all, she still had a mother's second sight and could read between the lines. "How's the remodeling going?" she said with a brittle smile.

You wouldn't believe me if I told you, Kathryn thought, but there was no way she was going to tell Sloane about her obsession with Rebeca Wright. *Or was it Rebeca's obsession with her?* That would be handing her mother a shitload of ammunition for continuing criticism, or worse, grounds for re-committal to GW Psych.

"You'll have to come see," Kathryn replied. A safe answer. She knew her mother would never again set foot in that place. "I'll get the shopping you left," and she went outside to Jack's Mercedes to retrieve the Neiman Marcus dress box from the back seat. When she returned to the house, though, Carmen, one of the housekeepers, met her at the door.

"The missus says you can leave it with me." She offered an apologetic smile. Sloane was nowhere to be seen. Kathryn almost laughed, but she gave Carmen a hug instead and handed over the box.

Moments later, she was back on the road headed for I95.

WHEN SHE GOT HOME, Alexandra Gold was sitting on the front steps, impatiently texting on her smartphone. It would do no good to try avoiding her, Kathryn decided. Her friend saw the Mercedes as soon as it rounded the corner from Wisconsin, and her flinty stare never looked away. Kathryn pulled to the curb and took a deep breath. Assuming a casual demeanor, she took her time getting out.

"Hey, you." She tried to camouflage her jangling nerves with nonchalance. "What brings you to the suburbs?"

Alex shut down her phone and stood up. "I have a client dinner in Arlington. You were on the way." The flat tone of her voice reminded Kathryn of the high school teacher who always criticized her writing.

"Time for a beer?" Kathryn chirped. Alex nodded without enthusiasm and followed her into the townhouse.

She was clearly impressed with Kathryn's restoration efforts and even more intrigued by the new furnishings. She didn't say anything, but Kathryn could tell by her furtive inspections on the way to the kitchen that her friend was appraising each piece like an estate agent.

"Where's the loo?" Alex said as they headed toward the kitchen.

"Use the one in my bedroom. Top of the stairs. Forgive the mess. I haven't made the bed all week."

Kathryn felt a chill as she watched her friend climb the stairs. *Wish I could start up the fireplace,* she mused. Why hadn't she called the gas company as Russell told her to?

"How's the stomach?" Alex said a few moments later when she came back down to the kitchen.

"Better," Kathryn shrugged as she offered Alex an opened IPA. "But I'm still downing Kaopectate like it's Jamba Juice."

Alex didn't find that particularly amusing. "We're missing you at the office, Kay. Some important people have been asking after you."

And his initials are WW, no doubt. "I'm sorry, Al. I've tried to stay on top of things remotely. I think I've just overstressed the system. Maybe I wasn't quite ready for the pressure."

Alex's neutral stare confused Kathryn. Maybe she wouldn't be able to bullshit her way through this. Alex was no Tami Frankle. Nuance and ambiguity were not her style. She got right to the point. "I hate to put it this way, Kay, and we would deny it in public, but you were definitely a lure in the Wright class action. It's still part of the game, even in this sexless day and age."

"Gee, you mean I'm eye-candy?"

"Don't be sarcastic. We know each other too well for that kind of crap. You wouldn't be on the team if you weren't first rank among the best and the brightest. The fact that you're brilliant *and* attractive to the right people was not something to be ignored. And don't tell me you don't get that."

"I get it," Kathryn conceded. *And that's what I'm afraid of.* "I just don't know if I still have the skills to manage it."

"I'm having trouble believing that. I've personally watched you verbally castrate a dozen Randy Raunchfucks and keep them on a leash at the same time. Where do you think I learned some of my best tricks, hon?"

"Well, maybe I don't want to have to be that anymore. And, by the way, why should I?"

This took Alex slightly aback. "Honey, you want to join HR, write codes of conduct and change the world, we'll make it happen. But it would be a supreme waste, as far as I'm concerned. And sooner or later you'd realize it, too."

Kathryn wilted slightly and Alex was perceptive enough to recognize the signs.

"But that's not what's going on here, is it?" she said.

"Excuse me?" Kathryn stiffened. Did Alex know about what happened with Jack? Did he tell her?

"Hiding out. Pretending you've got cramps. What's really going on, Kay?"

Kathryn was silent. Alex knew her too well. She might be able to con some of her colleagues, maybe even divert Tami Frankle, but not Alex. After a deep sigh she said, "Do you believe in ghosts?" A little sensationalist, admittedly, but she couldn't think of a more effective way to raise the subject. It got Alex's attention. She paused her IPA just inches from her lips and glared at Kathryn. Then, she started laughing.

"Honey, this town's full of 'em," she said. "Some are still walking around masquerading as congressmen."

"I'm serious, Al," Kathryn said with quiet certainty, keeping her eyes locked on Alex's. "She's gotten into my head."

"She, who?"

"Rebeca Wright. I can feel her. She's in my head. Reaching out. Trying to ... well, frankly I don't know what she's trying to do."

"Kay, the woman's been dead over thirty years." Alex's expression was darkening. "She ain't reachin' out to no one."

"I'm not making this up!"

The severity of Kathryn's tone surprised Alex. An uncomfortable silence descended.

"Kay, this romantic obsession of yours isn't healthy."

"It's not a romantic obsession, Al. I'm driving her car and all of a sudden I'm someplace I didn't intend to go. I hear music in the walls, cocktail parties going on downstairs when I'm in bed. I wake up to find all the furniture rearranged. Something is going on here. Don't you get it?"

Alex took a breath. "Okay, what exactly do you *think* is going on, Kay? What do *you* think she wants?"

"I don't know. Yet." She was now annoyed with Alex. It was an irrational anger, of course. Her friend was just trying to understand, but in so doing she sounded like Dr. Frankle. Kathryn wanted Alex to be Alex and say something like *"honey, you sound loonier than a cowboy riding a peyote jag."* Instead, Alex went over to the sink and poured out the rest of her beer. When she finally turned back, she wasn't dismissive, she wasn't upset. She simply looked sad.

"You're frightening me, Kay. I've never seen you act like this."

"Comes natural, I guess."

"C'mon, honey, this is Al talking here."

"Really? You're starting to sound like my mother."

"You know I don't mean anything like that."

"Do I?" *Shut up,* Kathryn's inner voice kept calling out. *Shut up, shut up, shut up. She's only trying to help and you're treating her like the enemy.*

"Okay, I think we should hit pause here," Alex said. "I've got to get to my meeting, and all I seem to be doing is upsetting you."

Kathryn suddenly softened and came over to take Alex's hands. "I'm sorry, Al. I really am. I'm just feeling a little overwhelmed these days. I've bitten off more than I can chew, apparently."

Alex's expression softened, too, and her smile became tender and affectionate. "Honey, I want you to take some time off. Forget about work. I mean it. I'll cover for you. No big deal. Get some sleep. Maybe even go away. Get out of this godforsaken place for a while. And check in with your doc. Have her recalibrate your fucking meds, for Chrissakes."

There we go. That's the Alex I know, Kathryn smiled inside.

"What about the class-action? What about ..." She couldn't bring herself to say the name.

"I'll handle Warren Wright. When you feel up to it," Alex said, "call me and we'll get everything back on track."

Kathryn leaned in to hug Alex and the two of them held on to each other for a prolonged moment.

"I'm not crazy, Al," Kathryn whispered into her friend's ear.

I am not crazy. Maybe if she said it enough times, it would become true.

But what if it weren't?

chapter
sixteen

The feeling of being watched was overpowering. It was the second week of her "leave of absence" and she had barely left the house. She let Russell go after he'd finished painting the second-floor hallway even though he protested that several items on their punch list remained unfinished. She pleaded limited funds and promised to call him back in a couple of months pending his schedule and her bank account.

She wanted for nothing. All her meals were delivered by DoorDash or Uber Eats. She spent her days reading or telecommuting to the office, submitting briefs and participating in discussions about the Wright Pharma class-action suit via email and occasional Zoom meetings, although she dispensed with the latter after Alex joked about her slovenly appearance during one session. It was true, of course. She hadn't showered in two days, nor had she bothered to get dressed. She'd been padding around the townhouse in her bathrobe, hadn't brushed her hair, hadn't bothered with make-up. She didn't even notice how disheveled she looked until Alex brought it up. Still, her contributions to the discussions remained cogent and insightful, so colleagues seemed to give her a pass. *Just another eccentric savant.*

She didn't dare ask how Warren Wright was reacting to her prolonged absence.

Jack had stopped calling by now, and that was a blessed relief. His messages had begun to grate, the apologies verging on the whiney. Her mother called once or twice or maybe even three times. Kathryn couldn't remember because she didn't answer these calls either, and she erased Sloane's messages without listening to them. But her solitude was being steadily eroded by that creeping sensation of being observed. Everywhere Kathryn went in the townhouse she couldn't shake the feeling that she was not alone, that she was being followed. She became obsessed with checking windows and doors to make sure she hadn't inadvertently left one open allowing someone or some*thing* to slither in unannounced. Unexpected noises in different rooms startled her, faint knocks, repetitive thumps, above and below, odd squeals that sometimes sounded like a child. *Maybe just a lost cat?* She could never find their source when she went looking. Sometimes Kathryn thought the entire house throbbed with a deep hum that passed through her like a chorus of neutrino oscillations, a subaudible moan she couldn't hear but definitely felt. There were odd, ephemeral scents, too, as she passed from room to room. A dizzying trace of lavender one moment, a tart breeze of lemon the next. Once Kathryn thought she smelled urine in the foyer. Another time the summery smell of gardenias mutated into an odor of rot so pervasive she almost vomited. She could never find the source of these either, and they all evaporated as quickly as they were detected.

That was not all.

Her skin began to feel too tight all over, as if somehow her epidermis had shrunk like a cotton shirt or a new pair of jeans left in the dryer too long. Her insides felt unnaturally constrained. But then, she thought, maybe that's because something else was competing for space in there. Another soul, perhaps, finally emerging from its quiescent chrysalid state.

Wanting to coexist.

Or dominate.

She was lying in bed reading a summary of depositions the office had transmitted earlier when her phone started ringing. She couldn't fathom the possibility that Jack or even her mother would be calling at such an ungodly hour, and she resisted answering it. It was probably just another of those aggravating robocalls everyone hoped had been eliminated some years back in the face of public outrage and government regulation but which had recently made a devious comeback thanks to the canny use of new technologies. The ringing finally stopped, which signaled the robot's capitulation when it discovered another digital entity had answered.

Seconds later the message alert chimed.

Strange. Robocalls rarely left messages. She glanced at the number on the iPhone screen. A 703 area code. Definitely not Jack. His area was 202. She knew because she had his number stored from the day she called to meet him at his gym and confirmed it by scrolling the recent calls list. This was a Virginia area code. Where her family home was. But it wasn't her mother's number. For a moment, Kathryn's heart skipped. It couldn't be her stepfather. No way. Unless he'd had some miraculous recovery which would go down in the annals of medical history.

She reluctantly tapped the message icon. There was an extended squeal of static followed by a voice trying to break through. The sound was akin to old shortwave radio communications one heard in classic movies, a fisherman at sea, an airplane pilot, a soldier on a battlefield trying to reach reinforcements hundreds of miles away. It was a man's voice, and it was hoarse and parched, like someone with a severe hangover.

"It's not fair ... the way you make me feel ... not fair ..."

Kathryn felt a cold finger of fear caress her spine. She had heard these words before, and the fact that they seemed to be calling out to her across an ocean of time only intensified her anxiety. When the static and voice were abruptly cut off by the message's end, the house got unnaturally quiet. She waited to see if the phone would ring again, but it didn't. She took deep breath and hit the re-dial icon, ready to ream out whoever was harassing her.

The voice that finally answered made that impossible.

"You have reached the corporate offices Wright Pharmaceutical. We are currently closed. If you know your party's extension, you can leave a message by dialing it at any time ..."

Kathryn dropped the phone to the bed and glared at it. *Wright Pharmaceutical.* If it hadn't been Jack calling, there was only one other person it could be.

THE NEXT MORNING there was a beautiful arrangement of gardenias in full bloom sitting on the credenza by the front door. She smelled them before she saw them and it flatfooted her before she got to the bottom of the stairs.

How could they have gotten in here?

The front door was locked. She had made sure before she went to bed last night. She came over to touch them, to convince herself they weren't some kind of mirage. *How could they possibly have gotten in here?*

She almost missed the small card hidden among the blossoms. It was yellowed and curled, frayed along the edges and filthy with smudges as if it had retrieved from the trash. *Or passed through veils from the past.* When she finally summoned the nerve to pluck it off the flowers, she gasped. It had a single initial on it.

"W."

Kathryn suddenly felt like an alcoholic in need of a meeting.

Warren Wright. It kept coming back to him. Kathryn was convinced Rebeca was trying to tell her something about him. But what? Roberto Gutierrez had said the night of her last Halloween party, something changed. Something was off. Things were different afterward. Rebeca got pregnant, Jack was born, and a year later she was murdered. Was it a straight line from one thing to the next? Was Warren Wright the connecting link?

Kathryn knew she had to do something. If she remained trapped in this competition between illusion and reality, she might, as she'd worried to Jack, succumb to the darkness again and become buried alive in a coffin of her own mania. She needed to put definition to these illusions. She needed to impose identity on the phantoms that were haunting her. She needed to satisfy herself that what was going on here was not the slow leak of her rationality, the inevitable, irreversible siphoning of her mind. There was a force at work here, dammit, incredible as it seemed, indescribable as it was, that was driving her toward some hidden truth, some dreadful fact that needed to be rescued from obscurity.

She sat down in front of the vanity mirror in her bedroom and glared at herself. She had told Alex she didn't know what Rebeca was trying to tell her, but she could no longer ignore the signs. Everything that had happened since she moved in here, every-thing that was happening still was pointing to Warren Wright. He must be the key, but to what? There was only one way out of this miasma. She had to own it. Take control of it. She knew how. She had done it before. She had to risk it again.

And that's when she picked up the scissors.

And started cutting.

chapter
seventeen

As soon as she walked into the offices of Brackenridge, Kelly and Levine the next morning, Kathryn could feel heads turning. Conversations paused, keyboards went silent. She figured she'd get some kind of reaction, but this was more than she expected. She barely had time to settle in behind her desk when Alex appeared at the door.

"Holy crap," her friend fairly shouted. "I heard you were back, but now I know why everyone was whispering."

"You like?" Kathryn smiled.

It took a moment for Alex to answer, and she couldn't quite camouflage her bewilderment when she did. "Well, it's definitely different."

"Did it myself," Kathryn laughed as she ran fingers through her short haircut making it look messy and chic at the same time.

"What possessed you?"

"Dunno. I was sitting in front of the mirror, getting pissed at myself for being so self-absorbed, thinking I needed to snap out of it, and I just picked up the scissors and had at it. I almost don't remember doing it. What do you think, really?"

"It's cute. No, more than that. It's sexy."

"Too much?"

"No, no. I'm just surprised. I've been hoping you'd bounce back. Guess I wasn't sure what it would look like when you did."

"Thank you, Al. You gave me the kick in the ass when I needed it."

Alex laughed. "Whoa, hold on now. I'm not taking the blame if you suddenly wake up thinking 'what the fuck have I done?'"

Kathryn joined in the laughter. "Well, at least it'll grow out, if that happens. Meantime, I couldn't let you down. So here I am, ready to rock."

"Honey, you could never let me down," Alex said as she came over to hug Kathryn. "I was just worried for you, that's all." As they pulled apart, she couldn't help running a hand over her friend's new haircut. "Remind me to consult with you next time I'm in need of a makeover."

All day colleagues at BK&L were friendly and smiling. They seemed genuinely happy to see Kathryn back at work, and they assumed her manic energy and exaggerated good spirits were the product of her few days off. She certainly didn't disappoint in the various meetings she attended to catch up on cases she'd been working before her 'hiatus.' To everyone she seemed fully informed of details and strategies and deferred gracefully to others whenever a sticky issue arose that required someone to argue a course of action that might be problematic. Several times she offered insights that tipped the balance in favor of one direction or another, but she did it in such a subtle way that made her point seem obvious instead of challenging.

Kathryn 2.0 was back.

With an agenda.

She fully expected word of her return, perhaps even her new look, would get back to Uncle Warren. It was only a matter of time, she assumed, before his interest would be piqued enough to prompt him to get in touch, so she could pursue her strategy and illuminate her suspicions.

She didn't realize how soon her refreshed self-assurance would be put at risk.

At four that afternoon she was summoned to BK&L's conference room on the west side of the building. Hot setting sun was flooding into the room silhouetting anyone sitting with their backs to the windows and blinding anyone facing them. But everyone's attention was directed to the big screen monitor on the front wall where a conference call with Wright Pharmaceutical was about to begin. Alex's assistant, Josh, was nervously trying to manipulate two remote controls at once, one to lower the solar screens on the windows, the other to complete the digital connection to Wright Pharma. They all waited patiently while the room darkened and *beeps* of internet handshakes emanated from the monitor's speakers. Kathryn tried to slow her accelerating heartbeat with steady, timed breaths. *Just like they taught us at GW Psyche.* She was both excited and afraid to see how Uncle Warren would react when he saw her new look. Would he maintain a poker face, or would she able to detect a disturbance in his composure? She leaned forward hoping the camera would focus and force the viewer's eyes to lock in on her. When the face on screen did emerge, however, it was Kathryn's composure that became disturbed.

It was Jack. He didn't say anything at first. His face dominated the monitor in extreme close up, and his eyes were staring straight into the camera lens in his office. He could have been looking at anyone in BK&L's conference room on his monitor, but Kathryn was convinced he was staring at her. Was he shocked to see her here?

"I'm sorry my uncle has been called away and can't join this meeting," Jack finally said in his best executive tone. "He's asked me to step in as his surrogate."

"We'll make sure a transcript of this meeting is made available," Alex said nodding to Josh who nodded back affirming the conversation was being recorded. "But I'm sure Warren won't need any elaboration of your capable summary." Jack seemed indifferent to the buttering. His expression was immobile. He didn't even blink. He just stared through the camera straight into Kathryn's soul. She was sure of it. "Since our colleague here," Alex nodded at her, "has re-joined the team from her brief absence, I thought it would be an appropriate welcome back for her to begin the update," Alex said. "You've met, of course."

Still no reaction from Jack.

Kathryn cleared her throat. She hadn't expected Alex to pass the baton, but *fuck it*, she was prepared. No way was she going to give Jack the satisfaction of intimidation.

"As you know," she began, holding eye contact with the screen, "we have filed several motions to have the class-action decertified, relying on settled principles that plaintiffs must first prove a pattern of false and misleading promotions that led to the over-prescription and misuse of Prolaxsis. Furthermore, that this pattern was deliberately meant to obscure the potential dangers and side effects of its use. We think we can successfully argue they have failed to do so." She felt good. On a roll. The words were flowing. No hesitation. She was firm but measured. Kathryn 2.0 was back, indeed. "However, we are simultaneously appealing for a change of venue from DC District to Kentucky's Eastern where a supposed cluster of major abuse has been identified. We want to argue the case ought to be heard, if at all, in a jurisdiction most affected by plaintiffs' claims. Now this may seem counterintuitive, but our assessment of the Kentucky Court is that its rulings are generally more sympathetic to standard industry practices and would be less likely to agree with plaintiffs' arguments that Wright Pharma willingly and brazenly exceeded those practices in the simple pursuit of profit instead of distributing a potential palliative medication that could help people. Abuse, if there was any, therefore, would be the fault not of Wright, but of overzealous doctors and or the patients that misused the drug."

Kathryn couldn't wait to get home and take a bath. Still, she never looked away from the screen during her entire presentation. She wanted to see if Jack would react in any way at all. He didn't, but she could feel the conference room relax as her colleagues clearly approved of her performance. When she finished, she sat back, still staring at the screen, and allowed Alex to take over and drive the conversation into detail and minutiae. For the next half hour, Jack just sat there and listened, interjecting only once or twice to have Alex or a colleague repeat a point or clarify the timeline. Kathryn was sure he never looked at anyone but her. And she never looked away from the screen either.

As soon as Alex wrapped up the presentation, Jack simply said "Thank you, all." And the screen went abruptly black.

Alex didn't need to compliment Kathryn. She simply raised her eyebrows. It was enough to say, "Well done, girlfriend." Knowing her, though, Kathryn was sure Alex was also thinking, "He never took his eyes off you, hon." But she didn't say that either.

No sooner had Kathryn returned to her office than a secretary informed her Jack Wright was on the line. She took a deep breath, steeled herself, and picked up the phone.

"Kathryn Fields." She used the most impatient voice she could muster.

"Very impressive," Jack said, and she imagined that charming smile of his. "You seem to be back at full speed."

"How can I help?" she said, maintaining her officious tone.

There was a pause at the other end.

"You could start by letting me apologize in person," he finally said, and Kathryn thought she detected a slight chagrin.

"Not necessary. I heard your messages. Your reasoning was quite clear."

"Do we have to be so formal?"

"I'm sorry, I thought this was a client call."

A disappointed sigh came through loud and clear, and Kathryn couldn't resist a small tingle of triumph.

"The past doesn't haunt us, Kathryn. We haunt the past."

"I'm not sure I know what you're talking about."

"It's just a room full of troublesome souvenirs we keep visiting to remind us how unfinished things can be."

She needed to redirect this conversation. It was becoming a little too intimate.

"I'm sorry, was there something we didn't cover earlier?"

"That report didn't change anything about you for me, Kathryn. I want you to know that."

She didn't answer. She was trying to fight off the temptation to relent, to soften, to give herself permission to start over with him. Handsome, sexy, damaged Jack.

Luckily, he was the one who ended the call before she surrendered.

chapter
eighteen

The past is just a room full of troublesome souvenirs. That's what Jack had said. He didn't care what she'd done or who she used to be, he said. *But some souvenirs recall terrible secrets, Jack, secrets that fester and corrode if you don't deal with them.*

She was living in a house full of them.

She had just stepped out of the shower when she was startled by the music. It was faint but unmistakable. Edith Piaf singing "Autumn Leaves." Again. The melody came and went, fading in and out as if from a radio with a weak signal. It didn't appear to be coming from anywhere specific, but wafted through the room like a breeze, sometimes in front of her, sometimes in back, sometimes above and sometimes below her. The effect was vertiginous. But instead of being afraid, Kathryn was strangely enticed by its familiarity. There was a filament of beseeching within it.

Suddenly there was the sound of breaking glass. Followed immediately by raucous laughter and a man calling out for more drinks. She went to the bedroom door and cracked it open slightly. There was a party going on downstairs. *Autumn Leaves* was playing on the stereo, its melody carried up the stairs on the scent of cigarette smoke and perfume. Women's laughter lingered in the air everywhere like canyon echoes.

This was no illusion. The townhouse had come to life.

Its past life.

Kathryn backed up into the bedroom and a peculiar calm swept over her. As if in a trance, she was drawn to her reflection in Rebeca's vanity mirror. The bloodstained photo of Rebeca standing between her husband and the image of her brother-in-law mutilated by Louisa Fedela was taped to the glass. People were right. Kathryn did look like Rebeca. From a distance one might even mistake the two of them. Without thinking, she used the Chanel perfume to spritz the air in front of her. The smell made her giddy, and she couldn't resist picking up the blush and lipstick. After two weeks of sloppy hibernation, she wanted to feel pretty, sexy, confident. For a split second, Rebeca's face emerged and smiled at her from the mirror. But this time, Kathryn didn't recoil. She smiled back, stood up and retrieved that black dress hanging on the wall.

When she stepped into the hallway, time slowed down. The light dimmed as if some off-stage technician had anticipated her entrance. The world became soft and gauzy. It reminded Kathryn of a theatrical technique she saw in college in which a scrim separated two realities. When the lights went down in front of a diaphanous veil and others came up behind it, one scene gave way to another. A parallel world slipped into the first. As she came down the stairs she saw two women hurry across the foyer from the study to the parlor, giggling, looking over their shoulders as if being pursued. One was wearing a long Victorian witch's dress, the other was dressed like a circus ringmaster with jodhpurs, top hat and whip. Each was wearing a feathered mask. A man chased after them carrying martinis. He was dressed in a white tailcoat and wingtip collar, and was sporting a pig's face for a mask. When Kathryn reached the bottom of the stairs, she passed by the coat closet where the distinct bumping and lustful panting of sex could be heard. But no one else paid any attention. In fact, no one paid any lingering attention to Kathryn. Her presence was not remarkable, apparently.

There were loud voices laughing in the kitchen. In the foyer, a crush of twenty or thirty people was lounging on chairs and couches, chattering in small groups by the fireplace or windows. Many were dressed in costumes or elegant evening-wear, tuxedos and cocktail dresses. All were wearing masks. Some were animals, some were distorted caricatures. Many were handmade. A few people had elaborately painted faces that completely disguised their identity. There were wigs of unnatural colors. One man wore a monk's cowl that obscured his face. There was a French maid, an Arab sheik, a Zorro, even a Saturday Night Fever Travolta. Several masks were explicitly gruesome. One was a featureless blank except for the staples stitching its lips together and the bloodstreams from hollow eye sockets. There was another with a phallic nose that extended six inches and poked at anyone who got too close.

Kathryn slid through the crowd, ignoring the small talk and laughter. She was aware of everything she was doing and was either helpless or unwilling to stop it. At the bar by the stereo a young man in a waiter's outfit and a Jack-o-Lantern mask offered her a glass of champagne before she'd even asked for it. She took it and drifted over to the window where the sparrow had been pecking the night she moved in. Outside she could see Rebeca Wright's silver Mercedes parked at the curb where she died.

A sudden chill swept over her and she turned away to warm herself by the fireplace. She watched herself approach in the mirror hanging next to it. Warren Wright had told her it hung there, and like a confirmation, there it was. Among the crowd in the reflection was a tall man in a classic tuxedo wearing that half mask that bisected the face from the left eye, across the cheekbone, through the upper lip and down the chin. The mask she had discovered in the basement trunk. Somewhere a voice kept calling out *"Robert"* over and over. The man turned away from the men he was with to acknowledge whoever it was. *This was Robert? Rebeca's husband?* He raised his glass to the person calling his name, and when he looked back he saw Kathryn. The half of his face that wasn't masked smiled. He drifted across the room and came up behind her, put his arms around her and kissed her neck.

"Darling," he whispered into her ear.

Kathryn felt like she might faint. The music, the laughter, his gentle embrace, all conspired to sap her will. Her eyes drooped, and she swayed in his arms. She was part of the saturnalia now, going through the motions as if she had always known how. She was familiar with everything, and everything was familiar with her.

When she opened her eyes, the man with the half face wasn't holding her any longer. Two men were arguing loudly behind her now, and a woman by the bar was angrily shoving a finger into a male companion's chest. The laughter had become brittle and ironic. Voices were too loud, but Kathryn couldn't understand what was being said. She caught sight of Robert again in the reflection. *It was Robert wasn't it?* He was in the foyer, standing alone, raising a hand as if summoning her. But then a breathless and disheveled couple emerged from their closet tryst and he vanished when they passed in front of him. Kathryn hurried out of the parlor just in time to see two women sharing a snort of cocaine by the kitchen door. She glanced into the study, but he wasn't there. Had he gone upstairs? She hurried up, stumbling as she went, feeling drunk or drugged or both. And something more. She was slightly aroused. *Had there been something in that champagne?*

"It's not fair, you know." He was in the shadows at the end of the hall by her bedroom. "You shouldn't be allowed to make me feel this way." He started to glide toward her, a blur in this dim light.

Kathryn teased him with a smile and slipped away into her

room. She could feel her pulse racing. Her breaths were shallow. She fell into the chair in front of the vanity and could see his silhouette coming up behind her.

"C'mon, darling, let's be naughty. No one will know," he murmured.

And now his hands were on her, caressing her breasts, pushing up her skirt, sliding between her thighs. She leaned back and pulled his arms tight around her. She looked into the mirror and saw that half face mask closing in next to hers. And yet, it wasn't her face staring back.

It was Rebeca's.

THE SCREAM of a siren outside woke her up. All of a sudden it was morning and the sun blasted into the bedroom through the windows she must have forgotten to curtain. She sat up too fast, and her stomach violently objected. For a moment she thought she might projectile vomit across the entire room. The nausea eventually subsided, but the pounding in her head didn't. Had it all been a dream? A dream so real it gave her a hangover?

She staggered into the bathroom and cupped handful after handful of water into her mouth. When she finally looked up, she noticed her Prolaxsis pill bottle on the shelf in front of the medicine chest. It was open. Lying on its side. Top off. Almost empty.

Alex's admonition reverberated too loudly in her aching mind. *Get your doc to recalibrate your fucking meds, for Chrissakes.*

"But I've stopped taking them, haven't I?"

Then she saw the marks on her neck. Large purplish hematomas. Love bites. Hickeys. The proof that she hadn't imagined it all during a Prolaxsis stupor.

When she came downstairs, the nausea lurched back with a vengeance. All the furniture had been moved. Everything was shoved around chaotically, sofa cushions tossed to the floor, a couple of chairs overturned. The lingering aroma of stale tobacco and leftover drinks made her gag. She went around the townhouse throwing open windows to alleviate the smell. In the kitchen she found a sink full of grimy dishes and dirty glassware with lipstick traces.

How could this be? Did a dream do this? Did she *do it?*

After she cleaned the place up and replaced the furniture, she went back upstairs for Rebeca's Walther pistol. For some reason she felt compelled to know how to use it.

She drove out to the NRA range in Fairfax. The place was shiny clean, almost sterile, which Kathryn thought was a bit ironic given its raison d'être, which was to help people practice bloody lethality. It was early and only a couple of shooters were there for the "leaded experience." A burly mountain man with several weapons laid out at his station who clearly knew how to use each one, and a grandmotherly type tuning up her defensive skills with a Glock, who pumped her fist enthusiastically after emptying a magazine into her target, all shots center mass. After explaining that she had "inherited" the Walther from a relative and deciding she ought to know how to use it, a cute staff member named Luke went over the safety rules and set her up with a box of ammo between Mountain Man and Grandma. After a few instructions, he stepped back and told her to "get the feel." The first shot would be a shock, he promised, so she had better be prepared. She should not, *repeat not,* freak out and point the gun in any direction other than down-range. Kathryn took a deep breath and leveled the pistol at her target. She squeezed the trigger as Luke showed her. After the first few shots, she was astonished at how powerful she felt. She dropped the magazine as Luke had shown her, reloaded and fired some more, this time without flinching. When she finally put the gun down, aimed down-range as instructed, she turned to Luke who smiled approvingly. An hour later, she left with a box of fifty .32 ACP rounds. The notion that this gun would be protection against the paranormal made her chuckle, but just holding it gave her an illusion of agency.

∿

WHEN KATHRYN GOT HOME, the front door was unlocked, and there was a man standing in the parlor with his back to her. She almost reached for the gun.

"It's like … stepping back in time," he said.

You should have been here last night, Kathryn could have said. "What are you doing here?" she blurted instead.

Warren Wright turned to her and beamed.

"I heard you were back at work. Good as new. I wanted to see for myself."

"How did you get in?"

"Your door was unlocked, darling. Not a habit I'd get used to, even in this gentrified neighborhood."

Kathryn just stood there and let him inspect her. It was so brazen she almost started to laugh. He must have realized it, too, because he abruptly broke his stare and turned back to the room.

"How did you know how to do all this?" he asked, gesturing around the room.

"I just put everything where it belonged."

"It's like it was just the other day," he murmured.

She brushed by him close enough to hear him inhale. *Was he searching for her scent?*

"I'd offer you a drink, but I don't have much in the house."

"Some of that would do nicely." He nodded to a bottle of Courvoisier sitting on the cabinet by the fireplace.

Kathryn turned to see it. *How did that get there? She hadn't noticed it when she was cleaning up earlier. Was it a stray left behind from last night's reverie?*

Kathryn kept her nerve and went to the bottle. As she poured his drink, she watched him in the reflection of the mirror he'd given her a few weeks ago. He was wandering around the room like a man transfixed, touching pieces of furniture here and there as if greeting long-lost friends. And in the flash of a moment, he looked younger. He looked like the young Warren in the photo with his brother and sister-in-law.

When she brought him the drink, his hand shook slightly when he took it. "Is something wrong?" she asked.

"A little chilly in here, that's all." He was studying her again, and she did nothing to discourage him. "They told me you came to see Louisa the other night."

This was unexpected, but then why wouldn't he find out? Warren Wright probably had influence in every nook and cranny of this city, and with that influence came knowledge, solicited or not.

"I found an old photograph of her and Jack," she said. "I didn't know who it was at first, and Jack made it clear he wasn't interested in anything I found. But I tracked down someone who told me who she was. An old acquaintance of the family."

"An old acquaintance?"

"Roberto Gutierrez." A spark of recognition flared in Warren's eyes. Just as Kathryn hoped. "I believe he was a photographer that worked with Rebeca when she was a young model. He said the woman used to be Jack's nanny."

"You're quite the detective, aren't you?" Warren said, trying to mask annoyance with a smile.

"I thought she might like to have it."

"The staff at St. Elizabeth's said it made her quite upset."

"Not that photo. Another one I found. The three of you. Rebeca, her husband, and you." She watched him carefully to gauge his reaction. "You were all dressed up. Like you were going to a costume party or something."

Suddenly, his stare turned inward. It was the same glazed look he had at her office the other day. He was being dragged into the past. But instead of the melancholia that accompanied those memories, this was different. Whatever he was seeing beyond the veil of time made him smile. And then, as if an abrupt gust of wind dispersed the image, his eyes refocused.

"Why would that upset her, I wonder?" He was fishing.

"No idea. It wasn't the reaction I was expecting, that's for sure."

He took a sip of the cognac and came closer to her. "Louisa Fedela is a very unstable woman, Kathryn. I thought so even back in the day, but Rebeca was devoted to her, and Robert was…" he paused, "well, let's just say my brother was not a confrontational person. When Rebeca died," Kathryn noticed that, like Jack, he didn't say 'murdered,' "Louisa became unhinged. Robert couldn't deal with it. We couldn't just put her out, so we made arrangements. And after my brother passed away, I continued to pay for her care. And still do."

Why is he telling me this? Kathryn wondered. *Is he trying to justify something?*

Just then a shadow passed over them. Like a cloud sweeping past the sun. But there was no sunlight, of course. It was night. And yet Warren appeared to feel it. The lifelessness. The cold.

"Are we alone, darling?"

"There's nobody else here."

"I thought…for a moment…maybe I heard…" He paused and looked around. "For a moment I thought someone was watching us."

Maybe it's Rebeca, Kathryn thought. *Maybe she's here watching us now.*

He reached out to touch her hair. "My god, you remind me of her."

This was the reaction she expected. It was the reaction she wanted. She wasn't sure what it meant yet, but a door was opening, she could feel it. If she was careful, if she was patient, he'd walk through it and reveal himself. She looked away coyly.

He pulled his hand back, as if he'd read her mind. "I'm sorry. Am I frightening you?"

Careful, don't spook him. "No," she said, locking her eyes on his.

"Perhaps it's you who's frightening me," he said.

"Now how could I possibly do that?" She instinctively lowered her voice to sound charming but not provocative. *Some of the old muscle-memory hadn't completely atrophied,* she was happy to notice.

Warren smiled. It was knowing, it was confident, it was appreciative. He put down his drink and put his arms around her.

"What do you want, Warren?"

"I'm not sure. All I know is the night I first saw you something got stirred up, feelings I thought were smothered a long time ago, feelings I was afraid I'd lost forever."

"Are you making love to me?"

"Call me old fashioned, darling, but I'd prefer the chase to be a little more prolonged."

Kathryn didn't back away. "What would Jack say?"

The question took him aback, but he was quick to accept it as part of the dance. "He'd be jealous."

Like uncle, like son.

"I'm not her, Warren." *Let's see how he reacts to that?*

"You don't need to be."

For a moment Kathryn was sure he was about to accelerate the pursuit and kiss her. He was handsome, self-confident, strong. Dangerous. She wondered how he would make her feel. Would it turn her on?

A violent noise interrupted the possibilities. Something had smashed into the window by the street and it cracked.

"What was that?" Warren said.

They cautiously approached to find blood smeared on the glass, and on the sill outside there was a sparrow quivering in its death throes. Kathryn gasped and covered her mouth. *Could it be the same one that was trapped in here before?*

Warren opened the window slightly and nudged the dying creature off to the ground. "It must have been sick. Disoriented somehow."

"I'll have my handyman take care of it tomorrow." What she was really thinking was *did this poor thing just save me from myself?*

"You're shaking, darling. Are you all right?" he said turning her toward him. "I could stay a while if it would make you feel better."

"I'm just tired, Warren. I think it's time for you to go."

"Of course. But what kind of a gentleman would I be if I hadn't asked." He picked up his drink and finished it. "By the way, how did you know Courvoisier was my favorite?"

"Intuition." She let him ponder that.

On his way out the door he paused for a moment to stare at the bouquet of gardenias on the credenza. He looked confused and turned back to Kathryn as if to say something but thought better of it and left the house.

She hurried to the door and made sure it was locked.

She wasn't sure she'd be able to resist if he let himself back in.

nineteen

Over the next few days, Kathryn kept a low profile at the office, supposedly working on the upcoming appeal briefs for change-of-venue arguments in the Wright Pharma class-action suit. She spent the rest of her time scouring the internet reading and re-reading articles she'd already studied about Rebeca Wright's murder and waiting for ... *hoping for?* ... a call from Warren Wright. Nothing could suspend her suspicion that Rebeca's murder was not a botched robbery. Something else had happened. Something involving him. She was sure that's what Rebeca was guiding her toward. And no matter how she tried to distract herself, she couldn't restrain the compulsion to find out what. And why.

Deeper searches with keywords inspired by her conversations with Jack, with Roberto Gutierrez, with Louisa Fedela, turned up a series of photos she hadn't seen before. Google images of Rebeca in her modeling days, at fashion shoots around the world, paparazzi photos of her arriving or leaving parties or nightclubs, posing on red-carpet affairs, even some Vanity Fair-type candids at charity events. But what caught Kathryn's eye most were the ones with Warren. These must have been taken during the period he was chasing her, according to Roberto Gutierrez, and they were fascinating for what they portrayed. An elegant young couple in exotic locations. New York. Europe. Monaco, Paris, Saint Tropez. There was even a photo of them on a Caribbean beach. Jamaica maybe, or one of the Indies. In every one Warren was gazing at her with an obviously infatuated look. She, on the other hand, was never looking at him, and though she was professional enough to offer a pose that was flirtatious, fun, even sexy, Kathryn could recognize the tension in her body language, the coiled posture indicating a readiness to flee.

One afternoon, instead of remaining hunched over her desk during lunch with a cold sandwich and a stack of law journals for company, Kathryn played hooky and found herself haunting luxury boutiques at City Center DC and Tysons Galleria. She had never been accused of being a fashionista, but the images of Rebeca Wright galvanized her, and she suddenly discovered that clothes and accessories she would have once dismissed as too chic for her instead intrigued her. She liked the way they made her feel about herself. Why shouldn't Kathryn 2.0 have a new look?

"So the haircut was just phase one, I see," Alex laughed when she noticed Kathryn emerge from the ladies room sporting a new pair of Manolo Blahnick suede pumps and a gossamer Ferragamo *birds of paradise* silk scarf.

"I could say it was my birthday and I'm treating myself," Kathryn joked, "but hey, why bother with an excuse?"

"Well, don't let the mirror keep you too long. I need to review Schwartz v Navy with you before the deposition tomorrow."

Shit, Kathryn thought, she'd completely forgotten that and was not at all prepared to coach her friend for the critical interview she had to conduct. "How's your four o'clock?" she stuttered, hoping to defer Alex's impatience. Alex nodded, and Kathryn hurried away toward her office to give herself at least an hour to cram some homework. She could feel Alex's suspicious stare watching her go.

The day went downhill from there.

Just before she was to meet with Alex, an assistant knocked gently at her door.

"Uh ... there are some gentlemen here to see you."

"Gentlemen? Who?"

"The police."

Kathryn froze. *What could the police possibly want with her?* She almost laughed out loud wondering if she'd shoplifted some goods while on her excursions. She stuffed down her sardonic humor and went to the lobby to meet two men who turned out to be detectives, not uniforms.

"Good afternoon, gentlemen. I'm Kathryn Fields. What can I do for you?"

"Sorry to invade your day, Ms. Fields. I'm Detective Ricardo," the first man said politely, simultaneously offering his card and extending a hand. He was soft-spoken, attractive, put together but not flashy. The good cop apparently. "This is my partner, Detective Franks." The bad cop. Marine haircut, high and tight. Bargain basement sports jacket and tie, and a humorless stare meant to intimidate. He didn't speak, didn't offer a hand. He just nodded.

"Could we take a few minutes to ask you some questions?" Ricardo asked.

"About what?" Kathryn said as innocently as she could as she glanced at Ricardo's card. *Metro Homicide Division.*

"Maybe you'd prefer to get out of the fast lane here," Ricardo said, and Kathryn was suddenly aware of colleagues and staff either watching this exchange or pretending not to as they went about their business.

"Of course. Let's go in here." She led them to a small glass-walled conference room off the lobby. She purposely left the vertical blinds open, as much for her colleagues as for the detectives. *Move along. Nothing to see here, nothing to hide.* She took a seat and casually gestured for the men to do the same. When everyone was settled, Ricardo leaned forward with an empathetic sigh.

"I believe you know a gentleman named Roberto Gutierrez?"

Kathryn felt the shrink-wrap tightening. "I've met him," she said.

"I'm sorry to have to tell you this, but he passed away last night."

"I'm sorry to hear that." *More than sorry*, she thought, but she put a grip on her emotions and held everything back. "What happened?"

"All signs point to suicide. It appears he drank a half gallon of bleach."

"Oh my god!"

"Not a pleasant way to go," Detective Franks offered with such deadpan that Kathryn was tempted to slap him. Even Ricardo shot him a hard look.

"When was the last time you saw Mr. Gutierrez, Ms. Fields," Ricardo asked while pulling out a small notebook.

"Uh…couple of weeks ago, I guess. I…uh…had tea with him." Kathryn's lawyer instincts kicked into gear. She knew not to be evasive but also not to volunteer anything. Let the cops show their hand with their questions.

"You were friends?" Ricardo continued as Franks bore into her with his steel grey eyes.

"No, I wouldn't say that."

"Then, your visit was professional?"

"Yes. No." *Dammit.* "I mean not in the sense that he was a client." Franks and Ricardo just stared at her waiting for clarification. "I was doing some research about an old case. I thought he might provide some insight."

"The murder of Rebeca Wright?"

So they were way ahead of her. *How did they know?* Her surprise must have been obvious. Both detectives intensified their stares.

"His housekeeper found him in his living room this morning," Ricardo continued. "She was very upset. It was not a pretty sight, as you can imagine. Among other things she mentioned that you had visited. She overheard some of your conversation."

"I purchased the Wright home in Georgetown. I'm restoring it. I was hoping Mr. Gutierrez could tell me a little more about Rebeca Wright, about the time she lived there, her taste. That kind of thing. Naturally, the conversation came around to her murder. He was very close to her, apparently."

"Apparently," Franks mumbled as Ricardo took notes. "Lots of photos of her on the walls." Kathryn thought there was something slightly lascivious in the man's tone, and he was definitely staring at her in a way she knew meant he was comparing her to those photos.

"Did Mr. Gutierrez give you any impression he was under stress?" Ricardo asked. "Any reason you'd think he was depressed, worried? Signs of heavy alcohol use? Drugs?"

"God, no. It was a pleasant conversation. He was a charming man, full of great stories about when he was Rebeca's, Mrs. Wright's, photographer and manager. I saw no evidence to think he was suicidal."

"Neither did his housekeeper, and she knew him a lot better," Franks interjected with that same deadpan tone. It drew another disapproving glance from Ricardo, which Franks shrugged off.

"Is that why Metro Homicide is investigating?" Kathryn asked as professionally as she could.

"We have to consider all possibilities. There was no note. The behavior seemed out of character. So far we can't identify any financial or psychological stress points that would trigger such a spontaneous and violent action."

"I don't know what to tell you. I hardly knew the man. I wouldn't be much of a judge of character in this case."

"We understand. But any tidbit can add color to the picture. In his reminiscences about Mrs. Wright's murder, can you think of anything that seemed to be haunting Gutierrez?" Kathryn stiffened at Ricardo's choice of metaphor. "Any feelings he could have been suppressing that might have been eating away at him?"

"Maybe something he knew about her death that he couldn't deal with anymore?" Franks added, and this time Ricardo didn't object. He kept his eyes riveted on Kathryn.

She decided to push back. "Except that it was an unsolved. A cold case you guys left on a shelf." She wanted to see how they'd react.

"We never give up on a case, Ms. Fields. We follow up on every new piece of information no matter how trivial it might seem or how late it shows up."

"Well, if he knew anything other than what was reported at the time, in other words a robbery gone bad, he didn't let me in on it." She watched Ricardo scribble so she wouldn't have to meet Franks' stare. "You think there's a possibility of foul play here?" *Let's get right to it.*

"We don't think anything," Ricardo said without looking at her.

"Yet," Franks added, looking at her hard.

"But like I said, it's our responsibility to turn over every rock." Ricardo closed his notebook. "So, if you think of anything he might have said, or did, even if it was just a wince at something you or he said, even if it's just a hunch about the way he talked or reacted to something, we'd like to hear about it."

Kathryn glanced down at his card and flicked at it. "Of course, Detective."

The men stood. "Thanks for your time, Ms. Fields," Ricardo said and shook her hand again. Franks just nodded, and the two of them went out the door.

Kathryn watched them go and tried not to meet the eyes of any of her coworkers, many of whom were now whispering among themselves.

Curiously, Alex never brought up the detectives' visit while she and Kathryn went over the deposition prompts she would use the next day. Perhaps she'd already gotten a rundown from others in the office. Kathryn felt the urge to bring it up several times, to reassure her friend that there was nothing to it, nothing that involved her personally, nothing that would embarrass the firm, but she always backed off. If Alex wasn't inclined to pursue it, why open a can of worms? At the end of their meeting, however, as Kathryn was leaving the office, Alex said, "Kay, you know I'm always here if you need me."

The non sequitur was so impromptu Kathryn wasn't sure she'd heard her friend correctly. But when she turned back, Alex was watching her from her desk with one of those smiles that simultaneously convey affection and concern. There was only one thing Kathryn could think of to say in response.

"I know, Al. Always."

The news about Roberto Gutierrez set her back. *Suicide?* It seemed so out of character for the man she had met. Then again who knew what kind of demons people kept locked away inside their souls, trapped and suppressed until their destructive powers can no longer be restrained? She could speak from experience about that. But to drink a bottle of bleach, now that was not simply putting an end to one's torment, that was meant to inflict punishment with suffering. At first, she felt guilty for even going to see him. Although she didn't want to believe it, she couldn't help wondering if she had somehow helped free his demons by conjuring a bunch of soiled memories, memories he'd been trying to outrun until they caught up with him at the bottom of a bottle of bleach.

Or could there be something more sinister at work here? Something that might lead police to consider homicide? There had been the sly glances between detectives Ricardo and Franks, as if they suspected something more than simple self-annihilation all along and were just probing for corroboration. They'd seen it all, of course, and something about this clearly didn't sit right with either of them. Or was that Kathryn simply poking around in the dark?

She got out of the Mercedes and started up the steps to her townhouse when she saw Ms. Dupree and Maggie on the sidewalk watching her.

"You cut your hair," Maggie called out to her.

"I did. Needed a new look," Kathryn said as the women came closer, eyes narrowing with concentration, looking back and forth between Kathryn and the Mercedes, clearly making a connection to the past and its horrors. "It's her car," Kathryn finally said, confirming what she knew Ms. Dupree was thinking. "A gift. From her son. He didn't want to store it any longer."

Ms. Dupree looked up at her with jaundiced eyes. "It's dangerous to imitate the dead," she said softly, then reached for Maggie's arm and left Kathryn there alone.

SHE THOUGHT she heard the *clicking* just as the mantel clock in the parlor finished chiming the eight o'clock hour. About the time coroners said Rebeca Wright was murdered. She was sitting in the kitchen eating leftover Blue Apron Caesar salad, and at first she imagined it was just the intermittent creaking of the house's old bones, or maybe a hot water pipe contracting. She'd grown accustomed to such sounds since moving in. But when it continued, she recognized it for what it was. A cigarette lighter opening and closing. The sound seemed to be coming from many places at once. Above and below her. Around a corner, right behind her. And then it stopped abruptly. Kathryn waited. It didn't start again.

She left the kitchen and went to the foyer expecting to find Warren Wright in her home again. But there was no one there. The house was silent. She waited. And still nothing happened.

Until the wallpaper peeled.

She heard it before she saw it. A ripping noise. Where the wall met the ceiling. She'd told Russell to paint over it because steaming it off would have been extremely time consuming, not to mention messy and expensive. Besides, he said, the paper was so old that it had become embedded in the plaster, fusing with it so as to be inseparable. Not anymore. A large wedge was curling away from the wall as if tugged by some invisible hand. Behind it, Kathryn could see plaster blistering, which reminded her of a frame of celluloid film stuck in front of a projector beam. Then the peeling stopped, and the blistering sizzled only a moment longer before it, too, ceased. She stood there dumbstruck, trying to decide whether this was a chemical reaction to Russell's paint or something more deliberate, more malevolent. The house shuddered and something fell into her hair. She shook it off and realized it was flakes of paint. She looked up and saw a hairline fracture cutting across the ceiling. It seemed to follow a path, zigzagging across the plaster until it reached the wall and started creeping down. Something inside or behind the plaster was trying to escape, something trapped under all the years of paint and wallpaper that wanted to seep into the present and become real. She thought about fleeing the house, but where would she go? Besides, this was her home, goddammit. She was not about to be driven from it. She wondered if she could get to the vanity and Rebeca's pistol before whatever it was got free. Step by quiet step, she climbed the stairs while the house shuddered. The seam seemed to follow her up the stairwell. Kathryn became afraid the house was coming apart. She tripped over herself on the top step but kept her balance and made it to bedroom. She got to the vanity and pulled out Rebeca's Walther pistol.

The cracking stopped.

Kathryn sat there and waited, unsure what she'd do next. The atmosphere suddenly felt thick and sticky, and a whiff of perfume drifted across her face. Chanel 5. Rebeca's perfume. The scent startled her and made her look into the mirror. Her face stared back, cleaved into shards by the earlier cracks. The effect made it appear as if she were wearing a hideous mask.

And then another sharp stitching sound began to scratch along surface of the glass. Another crack ran vertically up Kathryn's reflection, slicing the glass like a fissure on a thawing winter lakebed. Slow. Dangerous. Inevitable. She impulsively shoved a palm against it, pushing back against whomever, whatever was pressing from the other side.

"What do you want?" she cried out.

The mirror didn't answer.

~

THE NEXT MORNING there were no cracks in the walls. But the new fracture in the mirror remained.

~

WHATEVER WAS REACHING out to Kathryn was becoming more impatient. Of that, there seemed to be no doubt. The question was would she be able to figure out what it really wanted before it either gave up or decided to become more aggressive? Either prospect was alarming.

Being the good lawyer that she was, it didn't take long for her to track down the lead investigator who was assigned to Rebeca's murder investigation back in the day. Otis Stevenson was retired now, divorced, living alone in a small home he'd bought on the Magothy River inlet of the Chesapeake Bay not far from Baltimore.

And like a lot of retired cops, he loved telling stories about the bad old days, about cases he'd worked, the ones that ended well, the ones that didn't. Rebeca's case belonged to the latter, but he was willing to talk about it for the price of the lunch special at his favorite diner in a low-rent marina where he kept a small boat.

"I'm a Q-tip," he told Kathryn. "Can't miss me. Booth by the jukebox. My personal table. If you get there before me, just tell Marjorie who you are. She'll be the woman reading the *National*

Enquirer at the cash register. Don't ask her about the moon landing, or the Kennedy assassination, unless you want a lecture about how the Earth is flat. But definitely order the meatloaf sandwich."

Kathryn did as instructed and was sipping iced tea when he ambled in acknowledging the familiar greetings of waitresses and regulars and coming straight over to her. He was a lanky six foot five, seventy-two-year-old African American with gleaming teeth and cap of white hair trimmed neat and short. A Q-tip, indeed.

"Ms. Fields," he said flashing a thousand-watt smile.

"Kathryn," she replied and shook his hand.

"You order something?"

"Didn't get a chance. Marjorie told me what I would have before I even opened my mouth. Said both our meals would be out as soon as you sat down."

"That's my girl."

They exchanged a few innocuous pleasantries and she thanked him for taking time to meet with her. "I always loved the water," she said gazing out at the marina. "I can see why you'd want to retire around here."

He nodded and smiled. "I hate golf, don't play cards, don't hunt. Hate TV more and the internet most of all. Don't even drink. Can you imagine that? An ex-cop that don't drink? Fishing's all I want to do until the good Lord calls me home. Probably why the wife left. I was too boring." He didn't sound all that disappointed.

Just as Kathryn was about to get down to business, Marjorie showed up with two indigestibly large meatloaf sandwiches.

"I can already tell I'm taking half of this home for supper," Kathryn laughed.

"Really?" he said. "I always have a second one on order to go for that very purpose." And he proceeded to down the first half of his sandwich while she was trying to swallow her first bite.

"Wow, not bad, Mr. Stevenson," she said through a mouthful.

"Told ya." He paused between sandwich halves, drank most of

his iced tea in one gulp, then sat back to study her. "So, Rebeca Wright, huh?"

"As I mentioned on the phone, I bought the Wright home in Georgetown and found some old belongings the family didn't want. But they intrigued me, and I couldn't help poking around. Call it the lawyer in me." Naturally, she left out the parts about Jack, Warren and the possibility she was living in a haunted house.

Stevenson's eyes narrowed and he seemed to withdraw into his memory closet to open drawers of feelings he had locked away or forgotten he even had. "That was one of my first big cases," he mused. "Always stuck in my craw. The fact that it turned into stale bread. Didn't exactly propel my career, that one."

"Lots of robberies go unsolved, Mr. Stevenson. Especially muggings with no witnesses."

"Everyone was happy to consign it to robbery gone bad, but something about it just didn't sit right with me."

Just as she'd hoped, he was going to enhance the story, perhaps drop an insight or two that might enable her to understand what Rebeca was trying to tell her. "What about it?" she asked as innocently as she could.

"It didn't fit the pattern of the usual mugging. Yeah, her husband was beat down, his wallet taken, her pearls missing, but that neighborhood was not known for spontaneous smash and grabs or stickups. Also, in my experience, thieves don't hang around someone's house in order to rip 'em off personally. They wait until they can get inside and toss the place for all kinds of goodies. And even if they weren't pros, just junkies on a jones in need of quick cash, to attack and murder someone in a fancy DC neighborhood like that to steal a bit of shiny seemed so unusual as to be suspicious. At least to me. Neighborhood I came from bad guys didn't roll that way. And they sure as shit didn't cruise upscale zip codes looking for work. That was guaranteed to get you pulled over and harassed if you were lucky, worse if you wasn't."

"So the fact the pearls never showed up in the grey market, that surprised you?"

Stevenson nodded. "See, that's the thing. If it was smash and grab, the perps probably wanted to get rid of 'em quick. You stop by your local pawn shop and hope you can haggle the price of a fix. The Shylock would take one look at those high-end babies and kick your ass right back to the street. Then he'd call us and try to earn some brownie points. The mooks realize they don't have the skills or the contacts to fence something that hot. They'd have to reach out beyond their hood. They do that, we hear the chatter on the street eventually. Not this time, though. According to our CI's, those pearls were never fenced. Or if they were, it was somewhere way out of town. Beyond the imagination of your average DC mugger. Besides, even back then we had pretty good intel sharing. If something had shown up somewhere on the East Coast, we'd have heard about it. So, my guess is they were never hawked. That doesn't prove anything, of course. Maybe one of the bastards decided to give 'em to his Granny for Christmas. But it makes me wonder."

He ate more of his sandwich and she let him think about how he would continue the story. She didn't want to interrupt the flow with distracting questions.

"There's always the possibility the robbery was just a false positive," he finally said. "A way to divert us from the real motive."

"Which would be what?"

"Who knows? Revenge. Shut someone up. Drug deal."

"But you don't think so," she said reading the skepticism in his eyes.

"Those people, that neighborhood? Doesn't fit the profile. At least not back in the day."

"Jealousy?" she interjected.

"Possible. I suppose." He thought about it, then shook his head. "A crime without an apparent motive is the most difficult to solve. It was easier thinking robbery. But easy got us nowhere."

They sat there in silence for a while. She picked at her sandwich, he aggressively consumed his.

"You know you're the second person who has contacted me with questions about that case."

"Really?"

"Few weeks ago. Asking the same kind of questions, believe it or not."

"Can you tell me who?" She expected him to decline. Professional caution about someone else's privacy, or simply none of her business. Instead, he shrugged.

"The victim's son," he said between bites. "Jack Wright."

chapter
twenty-one

She debated whether to confront Jack about what Detective Stevenson said, about how he had been asking the same questions about Rebeca's murder. What other secrets was Jack keeping from her? Would he even tell her? How would he react? The longer she debated the angrier she got. The next morning she decided to end the debate no matter what the consequences.

Jack was working out with his trainer, Sean, when he saw her coming across the floor at the Equinox Sports Center. He became so distracted he never saw Sean's hard right coming straight at him. The punch caught him squarely on the temple. He would have become unconscious but for the thick headgear he was wearing. Instead, his mind simply got majorly scrambled for a few seconds.

"C'mon man," Sean said backing off, "keep your hands up. We're not here to cause early onset Alzheimer's."

"Break," Jack mumbled, and walked off to his corner. Kathryn was there waiting for him.

"I met Detective Stevenson," was all she said.

He spit his mouthpiece to the canvas and jumped down from

the ring. His expression made him look like he was about to hit her.

"It wasn't robbery, Jack. There was more to it. Stevenson has always suspected it. And you do too, don't you?"

"What is this, Kathryn? Some kind of crime groupie thing?"

"You haven't answered me, Jack. What made you start looking into your mother's murder?"

He shook his head. A sad, resigned gesture.

"You," he said.

"Me?" Was he fucking with her?

"You made me feel guilty. That day you came here, showed me the stuff you'd found."

She was having trouble processing this. It wasn't the reaction she'd expected.

"You made me ashamed that I'd been so indifferent. I don't know what I expected to find out."

"You found out the robbery motive didn't add up."

"Why? Because the cops never found the pearls that were stolen? That just means they were incompetent. I didn't hear anything that made me think otherwise. *Did you?*"

She pulled out the photo that Louisa Fidela mutilated. "I wanted to tell you about this the other night. At your place." She offered him the picture. He just stared at it. "I found the other half. It was stuffed inside a piece of furniture you gave me. Your mother must have hidden it there. I took it to St. Elizabeth's, Jack. I went to see your nanny."

"Yes, my uncle told me." He sounded more disappointed than angry.

"I wanted to tell you. But we..." Her throat seized up. She took a deep breath. "And then I found that file in your desk."

"Kathryn..."

"That's your uncle, Jack," she said pointing to the mutilated image next to Rebeca. "That's Warren. Look what she did to it.

The very sight of him made her crazy, Jack. He was involved. Somehow. I know it."

"Kathryn, you've got to stop this. Look what you're doing to yourself. Harassing a sick old woman in a mental hospital. Chasing down retired cops. Changing your appearance. Flirting with my uncle. All because of some weird fantasy you've concocted. What the hell do you think you're doing?"

"It's not a fantasy!" *Your mother is telling me so.* "Don't you want to know the truth? For your mother's sake? For your father's?"

Jack stiffened, and Kathryn could tell she was dangerously close to lighting a fuse she wouldn't be able to extinguish in time.

"My father was a weak, tormented man who couldn't stand the sight of his own son." His tone was so cold-blooded she had to take a step back.

"I can't believe that."

"He abandoned me. Emotionally. Left me adrift. I was only a kid. He begged my uncle to adopt me. God knows where I would have ended up if not for Warren Wright. He was more of a father to me than my own!"

She could feel Jack's trainer glaring at her from the other side of the ring. He was pacing and shadow boxing, but he never moved his impatient stare away from them. Jack must have felt it, too.

"Let the dead rest, Kathryn," he said.

"I would if they would let me."

His eyes became vacant. His shoulders slumped. She'd lost him. "Look," he said wearily, "I was hoping things could be different between us, eventually, but now all I want is for you to stay away from me, from my family, from all of this. Talk to your therapist. Get some help. But no more of this. Please. I'll talk to the firm about your participation in our company's class-action case. I'm sure they'll have other assignments better suited to you. I'm really sorry." He turned his back on her and hopped into the ring to rejoin his trainer.

Everyone in the club was looking at her now. She was sure of it.

What have you done? her inner voice screamed. He was going to call Alex. *You've just sabotaged your career. Again.*

She couldn't get out of there fast enough.

THE AFTERNOON AIR was still and crisp, and the departing sun lavished a crimson and slate glow on the clouded sky over the Lincoln Memorial that verged on the artificial. Kathryn was sitting on the grass near the World War II Memorial under one of those graceful American elms that border the Reflecting Pool. The pool's undisturbed water was a mirror, and the moody sky in it was a Monet. She hadn't felt so alone since those early days at GW Psych when she wasn't sure if she would ever get out. Reality had become inverted then, the way she imagined it was like on a bad LSD trip. She had known a couple of acid casualties in college who, even after intense therapy, never really seemed the same. There were those rolling eyes and disconnected pauses between thoughts, the clear indication of a slippery cognitive grip and the enormous effort it took to maintain even a fleeting relationship with normalcy. Was that to be her destiny? She had almost become resigned to the fact that her Humpty Dumpty mind had truly cracked in two and might never be put back together, that she was, in fact, crazy as a loon and should remain confined. But then, she found her way out of the tunnel. She reclaimed herself, or so she thought, until she moved into that townhouse and discovered ghosts there who were disrupting her equilibrium. There was no way to rationalize this, of course. Logic and coherence were inadequate to explain the things she was experiencing. It would be easier to accept Jack's notion that she was simply indulging some melodramatic romantic fantasy. What evidence did she have to the contrary? Only vague suspicions fueled by supernatural occurrence and coincidence. But despite her doubt, or maybe even because of it, she believed they were something real and true. Funny she should be pondering all this, she mused, sitting here among the spirits of this city. Their memorials were everywhere. What did Rebeca Wright have? A cold case file sitting in a box in some basement, a son who was content to forget her, and a murderer who got away with it. That was her memorial. The thought of it rankled. And yet no matter what she did about it, there was no guarantee justice would be served. If anything, the effort might destroy her instead. Talk to her therapist, Jack suggested. Right. The one-way ticket back to lavender walls, electroshock and clicking ballpoint pens.

As she sat there, she realized how tired she was. All she wanted to do was go home, start taking Prolaxsis again and sleep until next year.

GUSTY, raw fall winds swept across Georgetown streets tossing small dervishes of leaves into the air before scattering them capriciously in every direction. Ms. Dupree and her faithful housekeeper, Maggie, fought the chill arm in arm as they trudged up Reservoir Road toward Wisconsin. With scarves pulled tightly around their heads, and long cloth coats flapping like flags in a storm, the women mimicked refugee widows in a Brassaï photograph of postwar Paris. Kathryn couldn't help but admire them as she watched from her bedroom window. *Two tough old birds undeterred by the elements,* she thought. The wind made her windowpane moan, and she considered lighting the fireplace. The idea of curling up with a good book and her ghostly friends in front of a warm fire seemed very cozy, but Russell's admonition about leaky gas lines held her back. She made a mental note to make sure to call the gas company to inspect it. Winter was coming.

She didn't remember getting into bed, but she did remember

what woke her up. Edit Piaf singing "Autumn Leaves." For a moment, Kathryn wanted to pull the covers over her head and hide beneath the pillow. Maybe if she ignored it, the song would evaporate and the poltergeist that had turned it on would give up. She was too exhausted to confront another hallucination. Or was she too afraid of what she might see? Then the record skipped. Some flaw in the vinyl kept knocking the needle back. And Piaf's voice kept singing her refrain of regret over and over.

It became maddening.

Kathryn came down the stairs slowly, holding Rebeca's pistol. Except for the music, there were no other sounds in the house, no noise of a party, no shuffling of masquerade costumes, no clinking of ice in drinks, no laughter. She went to the front door to make sure it was locked. Satisfied that her mother, or Jack, or *god help me* Warren Wright was not making some impulsive, unwelcome visit, she moved into the parlor to find the LP rotating on the turntable, its needle skipping repeatedly over Piaf's lonely sorrow.

What would Jack say if he were here and witnessed this? How would he explain it? She could almost gloat. This was not just some hypnogogic fantasy, not some dissociative episode conjured by her mental fragility. This LP was real vinyl. It was really playing. And skipping. Someone had put it on. And it hadn't been her.

Whoever it was had carelessly discarded the album cover on the floor in front of the stereo. Kathryn put the gun down and lifted the needle off the record. The silence that followed was ear-splitting. It was as if the house was holding its breath. She was tempted to start the music again just to create some distracting ambience. Instead, she just stood there looking around the room, expecting the next spectral incident. When none occurred, she plucked the LP from the turntable and reached down for its cover. That's when she noticed an upper corner of the cover had peeled away ever so slightly. Like the wallpaper in the foyer a few nights ago, it was curled back on itself as if tugged by some invisible hand. Like a label from an empty pill bottle, or an address from an

Amazon delivery. Or like the infamous "butcher" album cover of the Beatles' "Yesterday and Today," the one where the Fab Four, in a grotesque tableau, were clad in white lab coats, draped in slabs of raw meat and cigarette-burned doll parts, sniggering like naughty schoolboys. That cover had to be quickly recalled when appalled fans and squeamish distributors protested. Maybe there was a similarly notorious original under Piaf's.

What Kathryn discovered when she carefully stripped the cover away from its sleeve horrified her more than any surrealist imagery ever could. A handwritten letter had been concealed there and fell to the floor. Kathryn picked it up and recognized a delicate and graceful handwriting that could only be female.

Warren,

This must stop! I can't continue to fend off your demands. You must finally accept that I will never agree to demean and humiliate myself more than I already have.

What happened between us at the party was unforgivable. I was drunk. You were someone else. But that is no excuse. Perhaps somewhere deep in my intoxicated consciousness I recognized it was you and had some inkling of what I was doing. Still, it was wrong, and we should both regret it intensely for the rest of our lives.

I love my husband. I will never love you. And Jack will <u>never</u> be your son! I would rather die.

You do not love me, Warren. Not really. Please admit it and act honorably. Do not break your brother's heart. And let me live my life without fear.

I'm begging you.

R

Kathryn's hands started quivering before she even got to the signature at the bottom of the page. "R." Rebeca. The implications of what she wrote were staggering. And yet there they were in Rebeca's own handwriting. The motive for her murder. The reason she was haunting Kathryn.

The envelope underneath the letter had been addressed simply to "W." No address, no postage. It must have been messengered. But it was obvious that it had been delivered, read and returned. Kathryn was sure of it because there was handwritten scrawl across the front of the envelope. An angry, masculine laceration of the paper in bold block letters.

NO!

There was only one person Kathryn could show this note to, so she left early for the office hoping to intercept Alex and preempt any other business from interfering before she could present her case. Rebeca's letter would prove that Kathryn wasn't inventing some preposterous murder mystery out of fevered speculation. The lawyer in Alex couldn't help but be intrigued. Whether she would ever give credence to the paranormal goings-on in Kathryn's townhouse was now irrelevant. Alex wouldn't be able to ignore the material evidence in Rebeca's own handwriting. And she would know what to do with it.

Except that at that very moment, Alex was being solicited for a very different enterprise.

Kathryn was coming down New Hampshire toward the offices of BK&L on the corner at DuPont Circle when she was startled by the sight of her friend sitting in a small coffee shop in the building's west corner. She was engaged in an intense conversation with a woman whose back was to the window, but Kathryn recognized the Anne Taylor jacket and Dolce-y-Gabbana scarf instantly. Her mother's style and taste. No doubt about it. Probably one of her recent Neiman Marcus purchases. The blood drained from Kathryn's face as she moved behind the parked cars in front of her for a better look, which only made things worse. As Alex's entire table came into view, she could see Dr. Tami Frankle sitting across from Sloane. And next to her, Jack! The women were listening to him in rapt silence. He was talking about Kathryn. Had to be. The only plausible reason this cabal would be assembled. This was how an intervention began. With a conspiracy of the beloved. There would be a calm confrontation. The sins of the accursed would be laid bare. Cajoling, urging, and pleading would ensue, followed by intimidation if those didn't bring immediate consent to enter rehab and treatment.

Nope! No way was Kathryn going to submit to that again. They could call it denial if they wanted to, they could say she was playing the victim card, but they would be wrong. Kathryn's heart pounded with bitter disappointment. They were betraying her. They were betraying Rebeca.

Fear and panic banished disappointment and anger. Kathryn turned around and hurried back the way she came.

SHE RETREATED into hibernation mode again, waiting for the other shoe to drop. Or maybe another sign from Rebeca. She wasn't sure how she'd react if the intervention cabal actually tried to lure her to a neutral place for a showdown, but strangely no one reached out. Kathryn figured Jack wouldn't think it appropriate for him to initiate things, and her mother was too chicken-shit to lead the charge. But there wasn't even a message from Dr. Frankle's office when she missed her regularly scheduled appointment. Maybe Alex had convinced all of them she should be the one to arrange the intervention, but the messages she left in voice mail, which Kathryn didn't return, seemed more pleading than coaxing. *"Kay, can you please call me. I'm worried about you."* The tone confused Kathryn. Shouldn't she have sounded a little less alarmed and a bit more chummy? Something like, *"Hey girl, no big deal, but maybe you'd like someone to talk to?"* Which was code for *"and then I'll drop the net."* Alex did come to the townhouse once. Kathryn hid in her bathroom and ignored the entreaties at her front door. *"C'mon Kay, answer the door. I know you're in there. Why won't you answer your phone? Please, honey, come talk to me. It's important."*

How long, Kathryn wondered, 'til they took drastic measures and called police to break into the townhouse with an "order to protect against imminent danger?" *We're afraid she is communing with spirits.* The possibility amused as much as frightened her. The fact that it was true was the scary part.

As if to confirm the Gothic horror of what was happening to her, a severe weather front was climbing the Eastern Seaboard from the Caribbean with gale force winds predicted to reach fifty miles per hour once it hit Virginia. Forecasters expected it to moderate over landfall, but DC had to prepare for heavy rains and possible flooding. People were encouraged to cancel plans and wait it out. Kathryn decided not to.

She sat at Rebeca's vanity and took her time paraphrasing the letter she'd discovered under the Piaf LP cover.

Warren,

I found Rebeca's letter.

I suspect I now know exactly what happened between you at that party all those years ago. She said it was unforgivable, and she remains tormented by it to this very day, even if you are not.

She pleaded with you not to break your brother's heart and let her live her life without fear.

You chose to do otherwise.

You need to make amends.

K

Outside, gathering winds rattled the windows. It was the perfect atmosphere for what Kathryn had in mind. Rain hadn't started falling yet, so she was hoping the courier service would deliver her note without delay. She gave in and took a couple of Prolaxsis to calm her nerves and waited to see how soon the shit would hit the fan.

Not long, as it turned out.

She wasn't sure what startled her awake. There might have been a noise, or a possible flash of light. Or maybe it was a pungent odor. One thing was certain. When she opened her crusty eyelids, there was a silhouette hovering over her. A man. Vague and insubstantial. Or maybe he was a she. A woman with short hair. Hard to tell. *This has happened before,* she said to reassure herself. As before, the figure remained immobile, indifferent to the fact that Kathryn had awakened to discover it there. She tried to move, but she was paralyzed.

This is a dream. A Prolaxsis inspired dream.

Something was weighing down on her chest. She was suffocating. In a panic, she willed herself to fight back, clenching her muscles into extreme tension. With a deliberate surge of energy she lashed out with arms and legs. That did the trick. She awoke with a jerk to find the specter gone but her arms flailing wildly in the air while her legs kicked spasmodically at the bedspread. It took a few seconds for her body to relax and her breathing to return to normal. The last thing she remembered was finishing her note to Warren then taking a couple of pills to take the edge off. And now here she was in bed. Had she passed out? Did the messenger come and take the note?

What was that smell?

She slipped off the bed and wobbled toward the vanity like a swimmer underwater. Her mind was fuzzy, her sense of self, disconnected. She discovered what the scent was. Gardenias. A small bouquet. That's what must have wakened her. It was sitting in front of Rebeca's vanity mirror, and draped around the base of the vase was something that almost made her faint.

A string of exquisite black pearls.

Someone had been in the house. In her bedroom! She instinctively reached into the memento box for Rebeca's pistol.

It was gone!

When she looked up, her fractured reflection stared back from the mirror.

And that's when the laughter began.

THE MASQUERADE WAS in full swing when Kathryn came down the stairs. She was wearing Rebeca's dress and had put on some subtle make-up. She had messed with her hair carelessly, and in a fit of sheer audacity she'd put on the pearls. She looked stunning.

As before, the parallel world was unfocused. Time was halting and the light was gauzy. Edith Piaf's voice on the stereo sounded like it was flanged. Mr. Piggy in his white tailcoat was still chasing Ms. Victorian and Ms. Ringmaster across the parlor, trying not to spill the martinis he wanted to tempt them with. The couple in the closet were still fucking. People in the kitchen were laughing, and in the parlor, people teased each other about their costumes, or were repulsed by the hollow-eyed horror masks with their stapled lips. Everyone was trying to dodge the guy with the phallic nose. Time sped up, then slowed down. Someone had her hand on the reality remote, fast-forwarding and pausing and rewinding. She saw a couple turn to toast each other with their cocktails, then suddenly start over and do it again. An instant replay. The party turned into a series of jump cuts.

On her way to the bar, Kathryn bumped into the French maid who was flirting with the Arab sheik. But as before, no one paid any lingering attention to her. As before, her presence was not remarkable, because when she finally caught sight of herself coming across the room in the mirror by the fireplace, it wasn't Kathryn she saw.

It was Rebeca.

She accepted champagne from the young man in his waiter's outfit and Jack-o-Lantern mask, then turned back to the mirror where she located the reflection of the tall man in his tuxedo and half mask. He was at the far end of the room with a group of other men. Somewhere a voice kept calling out the name, *"Robert."* He turned to see who it was and noticed Kathryn staring at him. He drifted across the room and came up behind her, putting his arms around her waist and kissing her neck.

"Darling," he murmured. She closed her eyes and leaned back into his embrace willingly, prompting a tiny voice to protest from the depths of her psyche. *"What are you doing? This isn't real. You're losing yourself."* But it all felt real to her, real and familiar. She was ready to drown in this surreal pond of the past.

And then, she felt him vanish.

When she looked up, he was in the foyer, standing alone, raising a hand as if summoning her. Just like before. But there was something wrong this time. Something different about him. Something subtle but frightening. She couldn't put her finger on it.

All of a sudden, a new addition to the ghost gallery appeared behind her in the mirror's reflection. Roberto Gutierrez, Rebeca's photographer and confidant. He was wearing a garish yellow suit, and his face was heavily made up with eye-liner and rouge. There was something different about him, too. He stood out from the others, but not because of his costume. It was the way he moved, the way he glowed. He seemed less ephemeral somehow.

"You asked me who wore that mask you found in the trunk down-stairs," he whispered into her ear.

A prolonged shudder swept through the room. Kathryn felt the tremble of past and present converging.

"They both did," Gutierrez said.

Her eyes followed his as they shifted from the man in the parlor to another reflection on the other side of the room. A twin. Same tuxedo. Same mask. They were mirror images of each other.

"Their costumes were identical that night. Just like them. Except one wore the mask on the left, the other on the right."

The image stunned Kathryn like a blast of arctic air. The masks *were* on different sides of the face.

"I suppose Robert thought it would be marvelous fun," Gutierrez smiled, *"watching everyone trying to figure out who was who. I can assure you I couldn't. I don't think anyone else could either."*

Rebeca's words reverberated in Kathryn's mind.

"I was drunk. You were someone else."

Kathryn sensed her consciousness beginning to slip away like water down a drain. She reached out and put her hands on the wall to steady herself, closing her eyes, lowering her head, gulping deep breaths of air in an attempt to clear her head and hold on. But the trembling of time continued. If anything, it got worse, crescendoing in a cacophony of growling voices, distorted music, and psychotic laughter.

The antique mantel clock above the fireplace began to clang with its Westminster chimes. Eight strokes. Each one louder and louder, more and more distorted until the sound became deafening. Kathryn thought the world was coming apart. She tried to grab hold of the wall because she was convinced she was about to be hurled into an abyss of chaos from which she'd never escape.

GW Psych, here I come.

And then there was a loud *BANG* outside, and the power went out. The house was plunged into darkness and everything stopped abruptly. The quaking, the roar of voices and laughter, all of it, dragged violently into the suck of silence. She remained at the wall, hugging the edges of the mirror, afraid to look into it for fear of falling into its vortex. Finally, she accepted the reassurance of the quiet and looked up.

The party had evaporated. The stereo was off. The furniture seemed untouched. The air was clean of tobacco smoke and perfume. All that was left were shimmering wisps of dissipating fog as the ghosts' lingering presence evaporated. Except for one. Standing at the threshold of the parlor, staring at her.

"You left the door open again," Warren Wright said stepping into a shaft of dim moonlight.

He was holding that half face mask in his hands.

chapter
twenty-three

I found this on the floor," Warren said. "More of your amateur archaeology, I presume."

Click, click

Kathryn watched him in the mirror's reflection as he reflexively toyed with the lighter in his pocket. She struggled to keep her nerves under control.

"Brings back a lot of memories," he said, fondling the mask in a way she couldn't decide was affectionate or perverse.

"I wasn't sure you'd come," she said. *Of course she was. This was how she planned it. If only she could keep her head clear. Goddamn pills.*

"What's a little weather," he shrugged, "when offered such a provocative invitation."

Outside the wind howled.

"Bet you could use a drink," she said, watching herself go to the credenza for the cognac. She could feel him moving up behind her.

"Transformer blew down the block. The whole neighborhood has lost power," he said.

She clenched her fists and dug fingernails into the palms of her hands hoping the pain would fend off the vertigo. Didn't work. The masquerade phantoms may have disappeared but she still felt time was out of sync. It was all she could do to remain on her feet.

"It's quite amazing, actually," he said.

"What is?"

"If I didn't know better, I'd say Rebeca herself had written that note you sent."

She turned away from her reflection and stepped into the moonlight. The sight of her stopped him in his tracks. His eyes widened and he caught his breath. His stare explored every inch of her. The two of them stood there, frozen like a photograph, each calculating a next move. Warren broke first. His posture straightened and the hint of a smile pulled at his lips. His eyes relaxed their squint. He moved closer. She held her ground. But the room was starting to swim. *Where was that fucking gun?*

"This is a risky game you're playing, darling." His voice drifted into a low, quiet menace. His eyes kept drifting down her neck to those pearls.

"I like risk," she said, offering him the cognac. "Makes the pulse accelerate. Besides, why play if the stakes aren't high enough?" *Careful. You're dangerously close to the line. Step over it, and you'll lose him.* He took the cognac and sipped, but his stare never left hers, and she could tell he was trying to suss out her game.

"You have alarming eyes," he said softly.

"All the better to see you with," she murmured back.

"It's not fair, you know. You shouldn't be allowed to make me feel this way."

She took the mask from his hand and leaned forward to put it on his face. His hand jerked up and grabbed hers in a painful squeeze to stop her.

"Oh c'mon, darling," she whispered as she caressed the mask. "Let's be naughty. No one will know." *Would he recognize his own words from all those years ago?* "Tell me what really happened that night."

His stare turned predatory and she could tell he was trying to choose between his anger and his rising lust. Perhaps they were becoming one and the same. "What if someone is listening?" he said trying to sound playful, but Kathryn knew he was considering the possibility she was setting him set up.

"The fear of getting caught always makes things more exciting, don't you think?" she flirted, fingering the pearls on her neck to provoke him. *Don't be afraid, Kathryn. He's weak. Coax him. He wants you. Make him show it. You know how to do this.* She slid even closer, pulling his free hand around her waist as if inviting him to dance.

"You took her into your arms, just like this. You confused her with your charms and your mask, and before she realized what she was doing, it was too late. Isn't that right? Isn't that how it happened?"

He breathed in her scent. He was on the verge. She could tell. She hoped he smelled only her musk, not her fear.

"A wise man once observed," he murmured, "that what most of us don't realize is that at the right place, the right time, we're all capable of anything. *Anything.* Rebeca and I learned the truth of it that night."

"And it could have ended right there," she said pressing herself tighter against him. "Your ego satisfied, her shame inflicted. But you just couldn't leave it at that, could you?"

He responded with an oily smile, and in it was the promise of violence. "How is this supposed to end, darling?" he said.

"With the truth."

"The truth?" he snorted. "What do you expect to do with *that?* Who do you intend to tell it to? More importantly, who do you think will believe it? After all, you haven't been the most reliable of narrators recently, have you?"

Kathryn didn't have an answer for that. She wasn't sure how much longer she could keep this seduction dance going. The Prolaxsis was wreaking havoc with her concentration.

"Okay, let's dispense with the charade, shall we?" he growled.

"My patience is running thin. How did you get these?" He curled a finger around the pearls. She saw something dark and dangerous flash across his face. He was surprised. In fact, he seemed suddenly confused and worried. Something was off. All along she had assumed he put the pearls upstairs with the gardenias, his cavalier way of confirming what she implied in her note, his arrogant self-confidence in the ability to control any situation. But now Kathryn realized he had no idea how the pearls got here. The Prolaxsis had confused her logic. Her assumptions were undermined. She had nothing to fall back on now but instinct and improvisation.

"They were…a gift." It was the only answer she could muster. She wanted to add, *"from Rebeca."* But he would never have bought that. She was having trouble believing it herself.

"I want them back."

"And if I refuse?"

"You should know by now, darling, I'm not a man who takes no for an answer."

The Prolaxsis continued to secrete its gummy paste onto her nerve endings. *Shouldn't it be wearing off by now?* She held his stare as long as she could while he awaited her surrender, but her knees buckled slightly and she staggered out of his embrace to steady herself on the credenza. She could feel her body start to deflate like a tired balloon. *This is it. Game over. The trap did not spring. He'll continue to get away with it.* He watched her with a queer, dispassionate curiosity. For a moment, Kathryn thought he looked a little disappointed, almost as if he was sorry the drama was about to end.

Then, all of a sudden, she felt something envelope her. A vaporous mist, like condensation off a warm lake on a cold morning, coalescing around her, glowing slightly as it shrouded her body before soaking into her skin like liquid into a sponge. Her expression emptied of life and transformed into a glassy doll-eyed vacancy. A shudder swept through her as an extrasensory presence entered her and seized possession of her will. She straightened up, stiffening and hardening like a fast-settling sculptor's clay.

"That's why you killed me, isn't it? You wouldn't take no for an answer. You seduced me, and when I refused to leave your brother and confess that Jack was your son, you killed me. Admit it, Warren. After all these years, admit what you did." Her voice dropped low and purred like a cat about to pounce on an unsuspecting prey. *That's not me, is it?* her own voice called from some far away corridor of her mind. *That's not the way I sound.*

Warren watched this transmutation in stunned silence. Had he somehow passed through the veils of reality into the realm of the fantastical? Was logic and rationality supposed to be abandoned now? He could hardly believe what he was seeing, and yet it was inarguable. Kathryn had undergone a metamorphosis more startling and provocative than simply cutting her hair or appearing in a suggestive black dress with a string of incriminating pearls. It was obvious in the shine of her eyes, the smile on her lips. He was paralyzed with fear and fascination.

"Who are you?" he said even though he knew. She was no longer Kathryn. She had become Rebeca.

She turned away and went over to the stereo where she retrieved Rebeca's hand written note from underneath the Piaf album cover. "I was weak and you knew it. But I came to my senses. I tried to make you understand," she said turning to him with the letter in her outstretched hand, "but you wouldn't listen, and you wouldn't give up. All you said was 'no.'"

"He's my son!" Warren shouted. "You were …" He caught himself and shook his head, trying to dispel this damned dislocation of reality. "*She* was going to keep him from me," he cried, correcting himself, still unwilling to admit the truth he witnessed standing before him.

"I've waited a long time to be finished with you," Kathryn/Rebeca hissed. "All these cold, desolate years waiting for my revenge.

And now I'm going to take him away forever. He's going to know the truth, Warren. And when he does, he will hate you. He will turn his back on you. He will curse the day he ever loved you."

She threw the letter in his face.

An explosion of rage finally overwhelmed Warren's astonishment. He lashed out with the back of his hand and drove her into the mirror. The shock stunned whatever was possessing her, and Kathryn resurfaced to the lunatic fury of Warren Wright's glare. He tried to rip the pearls from her throat, but she clawed and scratched and held his arms so he couldn't break free. His fingers grabbed her throat and began to squeeze. She went full-clawed for his face but he swiveled and parried her attacks. She kicked at him with her knees. He pressed her against the wall so she couldn't get leverage. For a split second she was sure she could feel his erection pressing against her groin. The violence of their struggle had aroused him.

His grip tightened. She had miscalculated. He was going to win. No one would ever know the truth now. He would dictate her obituary. She'd be consigned to the forsaken wilderness of Cassandras, pitied and disbelieved, a victim of her own absurd ravings and hallucinations.

Justice would not be served.

Rebeca would not find peace.

Don't give up. Not yet. It's not over. Not yet.

The voice called out from somewhere deep inside her, so calm, so confident and unafraid. Kathryn wanted to dive down looking for it, so she could be embraced by it, so she would no longer feel the pain.

No! Hang on. Only few moments more. Be strong. Don't succumb.

The voice had power. It galvanized. It incited. For some odd reason, Kathryn decided she didn't want to disappoint it. She opened her eyes and glared back at Warren with defiant serenity. She forced him look at her, forced him to confront her vulnerability, made him watch what he was doing to her. She made him aware of his own weakness. A look of terror swept over his expression as he saw himself in the reflection of her eyes. She reached up and surprised him by taking his hands and squeezing them even tighter around her neck. He tried to break her grip but she wouldn't let go. She held his fingers to her neck, to the pearls, and squeezed even harder. She refused to blink. The panic in his grimace intensified as something wet and warm oozed through their fingers. Kathryn felt a gush of something viscous cascade down her throat.

His hands finally slipped free of her clutches and he let her go. She slid down the wall to the floor as he backed away from her in horror. His hands were dripping with blood. He looked down at her in utter disbelief.

"What kind of witch are you?" he groaned.

She remained pressed against the wall, still glaring at him, still unblinking. The pearls around her neck were bleeding profusely.

And that's when Warren saw something move in the mirror on the wall above her. A dark figure in the foyer, gliding forward into the room, reaching out to him. He pivoted to face it.

Kathryn couldn't move. She could only watch as the specter floated toward Warren. A bright flare spit from its reach and illuminated the room like the flash of a camera. There was a deafening *crack*, followed instantly by a hideous groan. Warren's gasping body collapsed to the floor as he reached out in a desperate death throes attempt to reach Rebeca's letter lying a few feet away.

The figure slid into the shaft of moonlight and stared down impassively until Warren's gasps ceased, then it knelt down to check for a pulse. When it finally looked up to meet Kathryn's incredulous stare, she would have screamed if she'd been able.

It was Jack.

twenty-four

He knelt in front of Kathryn and studied her like an entomologist observing a new species of bug.

"You were perfect," he finally whispered. "Couldn't have gone better if I'd rehearsed you." He unclasped the pearls from her neck. She couldn't stop him. The Prolaxsis, the struggle with Warren, they had finally rendered her immobile. She was on the verge of passing out. And yet her brain refused to capitulate. It raced through the possibilities. *What was he doing here?* She tried to speak, but her larynx was raw from the fight. All that came out was a weak, incomprehensible croak.

"How did you …?"

She couldn't finish. She didn't need to.

Jack smiled.

"I've been here the whole time. Waiting for the right moment." He pried Rebeca's letter from Warren's stiffening grasp then sat down next to her and leaned against the wall. A rueful smile swept over him as he read what his mother had written.

"I was going through things to put in storage after my father died," he said as if to answer the questions he knew her mind was asking. "I found the Piaf LP and remembered my mother playing it when I was a baby. Maybe my only real memory of her. I noticed the cover was peeled, and there it was." He stared at his mother's handwriting. A strange calm came over him, almost a kind of relief. "At first I couldn't make sense of it. But then I discovered these." He held up the pearls. "Warren was in Bejing trying to finalize a very lucrative licensing deal. He needed some documents he thought he'd left at home in the desk in his study. I couldn't find them. But just as I was leaving the room to call him back, a strange urge came over me. A voice in the back of my mind kept saying, "Check the wall safe." Over and over. It wouldn't let go. What do you think it was? A happy accident, or," he winked and laughed, "maybe some paranormal guidance?" He finger-mimed quotation marks around the word "paranormal."

She was too weak to answer.

"Whatever. Luckily, my uncle is," he glanced over at the body on the floor, "*was* hopelessly old school. Same password for every-thing. His phone, his computer. His wall safe." He held the pearls up to the moonlight. "I think police call this kind of thing a trophy. Killers keep them to relive their experience. Sick, huh?"

There was no blood on the pearls.

Kathryn glanced over at Warren's body. His fingers were clean. She struggled to touch her own neck. No blood there either.

"Anyway, when I found these in his safe, reality suddenly shifted. Everything I'd believed about who he was, about who *I* was, it all came undone. For a long time, I didn't know what to do. My uncle was a rich and powerful man. He could have easily dodged the evidence. There was no smoking gun, or should I say, bloody knife." His laugh was brittle and bitter. "Any good lawyer, and he had the best, could have come up with perfectly plausible explanations for the letter, for the pearls. Right? You're a lawyer. You'd know how to do it."

Kathryn would have agreed if she'd been able.

"You wanted me to find them?" Her words slurred.

"Given how easily you took to all my other prompts. I was

pretty certain you'd decide to wear the pearls tonight and really fuck with his mind. Guess I'm a good judge of character. Right?"

Kathryn felt as if she was melting into the floor. She wanted to scream, but she couldn't summon the energy to drown out the implications of what he was saying. *He knew she had invited Warren to come here.* This had been his plan all along, she realized.

"I knew he did it. He murdered my mother. Or had it done. Same dif. He drove my father into alcoholic desolation. He took my family away from me. The man I loved and admired, the man I thought of as a father, he forced an orphan childhood on me."

Kathryn almost felt sorry for him.

"And then you came along," he said, turning to her with a truly affectionate smile. "I knew he'd be smitten the moment he set eyes on you. Thankfully, I had an overzealous private investigator look into your background. All innocent and on the up and up initially, but when I read what he'd found out, I knew you were the solution I'd been looking for. I would have given this place to you."

Kathryn's sympathy quickly evaporated.

"Why?" she barely cried.

"Oh, you can see it now, can't you? A brilliant but troubled young woman, a complicated personal history, incidents of mental instability, moving into a rundown townhouse with a dark romantic past. I figured you'd be intrigued. I counted on it. Your lawyer curiosity, your analytical skills. I figured all I needed to do was give you a little push. You'd be the perfect marionette. And you didn't disappoint. In fact, you've exceeded my expectations."

He was right. She *could* see it now. Even in the swirling miasma of her drugged state, it made sense. He had gaslighted her. And she had risen to the bait. Willingly. Enthusiastically.

"Her vanity, behind the wall," she managed to say.

"I thought that was kind of inspired, don't you? Really got the ball rolling. You made my mother's dress look like a work of art, by the way."

Kathryn felt like she might throw up. *What must he have been thinking while he made love to me?*

"I started letting myself in while you were sleeping, moving things around, playing music at all hours. That was the easy part. Especially since I made sure your Prolaxsis exceeded the dose your doctor prescribed. By a lot. Then, I started leaving other things for you to find. The cognac. The mask. The Piaf LP with my mother's letter. You took it from there. I've been truly fascinated by your initiative, your ingenuity. Things I hadn't even thought of. The visit to Louisa at St. E's. Your conversations with Gutierrez, with Detective Stevenson. Although I must admit, Gutierrez was a little problematic. You stirred up a lot of memories. He called me. Said some things were coming back to him. I had to nip that one in the bud."

Oh God. He killed Roberto. And it's my fault.

"Please, stop," she moaned. She couldn't take the indictment any longer. How could she have been so malleable? How could she have allowed herself to be manipulated so cunningly? How did she not see the psychopath lurking behind his charm?

"Don't feel guilty, Kathryn. Warren got away with it for over thirty years. And he would have gotten away with it forever. But now, you've brought him to justice."

"Me?"

"Of course, darling. Everyone knows you've been obsessed with what happened to my mother. Who knows what was going through your crazed imagination when my uncle came here tonight? By the way, how many Prolaxsis have you taken?"

Is he smiling?

Jack reached into his pocket for a handkerchief. And now she noticed that he was holding Rebeca's pistol from the memento box upstairs. He wiped it down and placed it in her right hand. For a moment, she contemplated using it on him.

She willed her fingers to go limp and drop the gun, but it was too late. Her fingerprints were on it now. Her muscles quivered as she struggled to aim it at him. He just stood there and watched.

CLICK CLICK

She managed to pull the trigger.

He didn't even flinch.

"You don't think I'd hand you a loaded gun, do you?"

There was that smile again. The one that had once seemed so charming but now just looked smug. He shrugged and got to his feet.

"Only a few minor loose ends to clean up," he said as he held up his mother's letter. "I think this might confuse the issue, don't you? Beg some questions we really don't want to have to deal with. Best to be rid of it, I think." He reached into Warren's pocket for his lighter, then walked over to the fireplace.

Kathryn tried to shift her body against the wall. Something was clawing at her, something in the depths of her mind, something urgent that was crying out for attention. It felt like a warning, but the cacophony of everything that had just happened was drowning it out. Jack leaned down and found the key to the fireplace gas feed. The alarm in her mind was shouting louder and louder. He tossed Rebeca's letter on to the grate and turned the key. He flicked Warren's lighter, but it wouldn't ignite. She tried to move but her body was too rubbery. Her thoughts sent commands to muscles that ignored or diverted them. Her limbs moved in ways she didn't intend.

Have to get out of here, her inner voice screamed. She clawed at the floor trying to drag herself away. *Have to get out of this room.*

Jack didn't hear her. He kept grinding the lighter's flint trying to get it to ignite. Kathryn's body finally failed her and she fell over to her side with a loud groan.

This time he heard her and turned. Just as the lighter's wick finally caught. And in that instant Kathryn saw the gas pipe explode. A jet of fire sprayed out and Rebeca's letter ignited like a piece of flashpaper. The pipe became a flamethrower and spewed fire into the room. A flare was ejected and seized Jack's arm. He danced away in shock and terror as the flame raced toward his face. *This can't be happening,* Kathryn thought. *This is not real.*

But it was real.

Jack was now a human torch jerking about in palsied agony, grabbing for curtains and furniture, igniting them with his touch, his mouth agape with silent screams, his hands beating against his blistering skin in a futile attempt to stifle the blazing cocoon that was consuming him.

Soon the whole room was on fire. Kathryn started to gag as smoke curled around her, but she couldn't rouse herself to escape. Her adrenaline was not enough to overcome the anesthesia of the drug contaminating her blood. Across the room, Jack stopped and turned toward her. His arms reached out in a pathetic plea for help, or mercy. And then he toppled over like a felled tree. He landed next to his uncle where he trembled for a moment then went still.

The fire roared like a raging animal. Or a triumphant one.

Kathryn's eyes stung and watered. She couldn't decide if she was crying or simply reacting to the smoke. Strangely, she wasn't afraid, she wasn't sad. In fact, she didn't feel anything.

Is that the Prolaxsis? she thought.

The last thing she saw was a pillar of smokeless flame coalescing in the center of the room, a fiery dervish that seemed to manifest spontaneously in the air to hover above Jack and Warren's bodies. It bent over them as if staring down, growing larger and brighter, becoming blindingly white and radiant. Kathryn couldn't catch her breath. The cyclone of fire was consuming all the oxygen in the room. Finally, it straightened up and turned to her. It had a shape now, female, and a face forming in the inferno. It smiled gently, and Kathryn heard its voice in her mind. Somehow she understood that something was being asked of her. She couldn't reply with her voice, so her mind did instead. And she promised. She promised to do what Rebeca asked.

As she closed her eyes to let go, she felt the fire tugging at her. Pulling at her arms and legs, dragging her across the room. She was a limp doll. Couldn't open her eyes. Couldn't resist.

And she didn't care. She slipped away into a quiet, insensate darkness.

twenty-five

C lick click click.

If Frankle doesn't stop playing with that goddamned pen, I'm going to yank it from her hands and break it in two.

Then pain intervened. It dragged Kathryn back to the surface of consciousness, away from the hallucination of her psychiatrist's office, back to the hospital room where she found her therapist slouched in a chair, staring out at an aluminum blanket of sky, lost in thought, notepad in hand, mindlessly clicking away, doing penance for her role in this whole mess, ever since the CSI had analyzed the meds they found in Kathryn's bathroom. To Frankle's horror, Kathryn's Prolaxsis turned out to be triple the dosage she had prescribed. Such a high dose would have been meant only for clinical situations with acute bipolar or schizophrenic patients. Side effects would be severe in typical ambulatory treatment. Intense hallucinations, memory loss, and time distortion would almost certainly occur. Neither Frankle nor Kathryn's druggist could account for this terrible discrepancy. The only likely explanation was a manufacturer's batch that had been mislabeled. Frankle was almost frantic with apology, and Kathryn couldn't decide if she was begging forgiveness or pleading for no lawsuit. Maybe both. But Kathryn was too out of it to care. It didn't matter anyway. She knew exactly how she ended up overdosing on Prolaxsis. Jack had switched the pills. He certainly had the wherewithal to do so. It was probably the night she first went out with him, when he found her upstairs and unconscious. He likely took the opportunity to replace hers with ones he knew would drive her crazy. Sooner or later.

"How long have you been there?" Kathryn croaked.

Frankle abruptly reinflated her posture and assumed a professional smile. "Only a few minutes," she said as she bound out of her chair to deliver the sippy cup and straw that was on the bedside table.

Kathryn had been weaned off the "mercy flow" of her morphine drip last night, and her wrists felt like they were bound by barbed wire. At least the swelling in her ankles had retreated, and the skin grafts around them were finally adhering. *It took only two tries, for Chrissake.* They still itched like hell, but nurses assured her she would soon be able to walk without a cane.

"I told your mother to go home and get some rest. I'd stay with you until Alex got here with the police."

The police. Franks and Ricardo. The detectives who had questioned her after Roberto Gutierrez's death.

Not suicide, fellas. Murder! Jack killed him. But you'll never know that now. I made a promise.

When Kathryn woke up in ICU at Georgetown University Hospital, she couldn't remember what had happened to her. She was surrounded by doctors who were jamming a bronchoscope down her throat while her mother and Alex, sequestered beyond plate glass walls, watched with barely controlled panic. The Propofol Kathryn's doctors administered turned her world into a magical mystery tour. The next few days were a blur of distorted faces and fever dreams. Alex stepped in and took charge, running interference with the press, mollifying Kathryn's frantic mother, interrogating doctors relentlessly, and keeping Franks and Ricardo at bay.

Thank God for Alex.

"Paramedics had one hell of a time keeping you breathing, girl," she had said. "You must have inhaled the equivalent of a couple of cartons of cigarettes. Docs thought it was touch and go there for a while." Exactly when Alex told her all this, Kathryn couldn't remember. In her semi-lucid moments, she tried to tell her friend what had happened, but the damage to her throat and lungs prevented her from getting more than a few cryptic phrases out. Thankfully, Kathryn thought, because she needed time to compose a narrative slightly different from the actual truth, a narrative that wouldn't contradict whatever she'd said at the scene while she was barely coherent. She hoped the police would buy it.

"WELL, well, there's the girl I know," Alex said, sweeping into the room like a gust of wind, ignoring Dr. Frankle and bringing an elaborate arrangement of cut flowers for Kathryn to smell. When she sensed Tami Frankle's raised eyebrow, she added, "Docs said it was okay," and pulled Kathryn's oxygen cannula away so she could take a good whiff.

"Gardenias," Kathryn rasped.

"The guys at the office said they were your favorite."

Warren Wright's favorite, Kathryn wanted to say, but she let the irony pass with a weak smile. "The police?" she whispered.

"Don't worry about them. I've got 'em corralled like couple of fresh cut steers." Alex could feel Tami Frankle shifting in her chair on the other side of the room. "You don't feel like answering, just give me a high sign. I'll manage 'em." More shifting across the room. Alex turned to Frankle. "And I'll fill you in later, after they leave."

"I'll be in the waiting room," Frankle nodded, but it was clear she didn't appreciate being "managed."

WHEN RICARDO and Franks finally arrived, Kathryn had fallen asleep again. She'd been dreaming about fire, about Warren Wright dead on the floor and Jack jerking around the room in his death dance. She dreamt of the flaming djinni with Rebeca's face levitating over them, then turning to her and smiling, at once grateful and beseeching, as if it were thanking Kathryn but also hoping she would somehow safeguard the reality of what really happened. In her dream, Kathryn promised again to keep the secret.

Ricardo and Franks were no dream.

"We're sorry to have to bother you, Ms. Fields, and," with a glance toward Alex, "we appreciate your attorney's cooperation."

Kathryn only nodded. The less she had to say the better, both for her throat and her conscience.

"Feel up to a few questions?"

Kathryn nodded again, and Ricardo pulled out a small notebook.

"When your neighbor and her housekeeper found you on the floor in the foyer of your townhouse, you told them you'd been assaulted. That right?"

"Did I?" Kathryn whispered. Actually, she had no idea what she'd said to anyone. She didn't remember anything. She had been delirious.

"They'd heard banging next door and saw the glow of flames coming from your house," Ricardo continued. "Your front door was ajar. Your body was on the floor just inside. They got you out."

So, old Ms. Dupree and her faithful pal, Maggie, had saved her life.

"And the man who assaulted you was still in the building?"

"Yes."

"And there was someone else there, too."

Kathryn's eyes began to fill up. "Jack." She said his name so quietly Ricardo leaned in closer to make sure.

"Jack Wright?"

"Yes."

"The parlor was fully engulfed in fire when Ms. Dupree and her housekeeper found you," Ricardo said checking his notes.

"Fire department said it was like the furnace of a crematorium," Detective Franks added.

Ever tactful, that one.

"It took the ME quite a while to identify the bodies," Ricardo continued. "But he confirmed the deceased were, in fact, Jack Wright and his uncle Warren Wright." He paused to clock Kathryn's reaction. "Which one was it that assaulted you?"

"We've already gone over this, Detectives," Alex interjected.

"We need to hear it from Ms. Fields," Franks shot back.

"Warren. It was Warren. He was pursuing me," Kathryn said. "Wouldn't take no for an answer."

"I've provided phone logs to confirm Warren Wright's obsession with my colleague," Alex said.

"And his nephew interrupted the...assault."

"Yes."

"And he was there, why?"

Kathryn paused and took a deep breath. "He and I...we'd been intimate. I told him about his uncle." *True enough. Please, let it be enough.*

The answer didn't fully satisfy Ricardo or Franks, but Ricardo pressed on.

"And in the struggle, a gun went off."

"Yes."

"Whose gun?"

"Rebeca's," Kathryn said after a pregnant pause.

This confused Ricardo, or he pretended it did. He glanced over at Franks who shrugged skeptically.

"Rebeca Wright, gentlemen," Alex jumped in. "Again, I've provided Ms. Field's statement to the effect. It was left behind with some forgotten personal belongings when the townhouse was sold. Kathryn offered to return it to her son, Jack Wright, but he declined to accept it. Subsequently, it was duly registered as hers."

"And you kept it handy," Ricardo stated, making a note.

"And loaded," Franks monotoned.

"In the parlor," Kathryn said haltingly. "To deter Warren. He had been sneaking into my house. He got it away from me. It went off in the struggle when Jack intervened."

"Yes, we have..." checking his notes, "Ms. Geraldine Dupree's statement, supported by her housekeeper, a Miss Margaret Cork, that she witnessed Mr. Wright entering your townhouse on several occasions prior to this incident."

"And that's when you escaped?" Franks asked.

"No. After the fire started."

Detective Franks now leaned forward slightly. Apparently, this is where he hoped the story got good. "Investigators say a leak in the gas feed to the fireplace ignited," he said.

"That's in their report," Alex sighed to make clear her growing impatience.

Ricardo ignored her. "Any idea why it would ignite at that very moment?" Again, boring in on Kathryn.

"It was Jack. Power was out. The storm. He wanted to light a candle. Wait for police. We didn't know...he didn't mean to ..." She didn't finish. The image of Jack aflame finally brought on the tears.

Alex seized the opportunity. "Okay, boys, that's enough for now." She could tell Franks was ready to push on, but Ricardo chose discretion. He folded up his notebook and stood.

"Thank you, Ms. Fields. We'll be in touch if there's anything further. Glad your wounds are limited to wrists and ankles."

The way he said this made Kathryn think he was suspicious.

As the two men made their way to the door, Franks paused and turned back. "By the way, how did you get to the foyer where the Dupree woman and her housekeeper found you?"

Kathryn just shook her head. *You wouldn't believe me if I told you.*

"Should be able to move back into your home soon," Ricardo said trying to sound genuine. "Not a scorch anywhere else in the house. Just the parlor." Again, that subtext of suspicion. The detectives stared at Kathryn to see how she reacted. Clearly, they thought it was unusual. Wonder what she thought?

"We've got a great fire department, don't we," Alex said holding the door open for them.

MERCIFULLY, Ricardo and Franks left it at that. Kathryn's narrative was the only source of information about what happened. There was no forensic evidence to contradict it. The fire took care of that. Since Warren Wright was deceased, there was no longer a criminal case to be investigated. "De motuis nihil nisi bonum." Literally, "of the dead, nothing that is not good." Or more prosaically, "let the dead bury their own." True to form, lawyers and PR flaks at Wright Pharmaceutical went into overdrive. After negotiations with Alex, Wright Pharma agreed to a substantial settlement if Kathryn would sign a non-disclosure agreement and refuse to make any public comments about what happened that night. Kathryn agreed without hesitation. She couldn't care less about the money.

And there was the promise that she'd made to Rebeca.

"You sure you want to stay here? After all that's happened?" Alex said later. They were alone in the kitchen of Kathryn's townhouse nursing a couple of beers, trying to ignore the creosote stench still permeating the atmosphere.

"It's my home, Al."

"It's remarkable," Alex said, looking around. "The rest of this place left unscathed. Miraculous, really."

"Russell says he and his crew can finish the renovations in a few weeks." She couldn't stop rubbing her wrists, but at least her ankles didn't itch any longer. She'd be able to ditch the cane in a week, doctors said.

"What about your ghost?" Alex said half-jokingly, but Kathryn knew she was probing.

Kathryn played along. "Haven't heard from her. Guess she got bored."

Alex accepted the evasion. A little reluctantly, Kathryn thought. She never took her eyes off Kathryn as she pushed paperwork on the table toward her and offered a pen.

Kathryn scribbled her signature on NDA from Wright Pharma, endorsed the check and slid it back across the table as if it were toxic. Alex shoved it into her briefcase without comment. She'd already made arrangements for the money to be donated to the Battered Women's Project as per Kathryn's expressed wishes.

"I'm so sorry, Kay," Alex sighed on the verge of tears. "I should have seen it coming. I never should have put you in such a vulnerable situation."

Kathryn tried to reassure her by taking her hands and holding them tight. What was there to say? What would her best friend think if she knew Kathryn had deliberately chosen to exploit that very vulnerability?

"I should have listened to you. But I let my ambition for the firm overrule my better judgment," Alex continued.

Kathryn didn't argue. The truth was far more complicated. More than she would ever confess to Alex. And Alex seemed to sense this. Kathryn could feel it, reading between the lines of their conversation, hidden behind her friend's long stares. But Alex let it go. Perhaps she really didn't want to know.

De mortuis nihil nisi bonum. Let the dead bury their own.

They finished their beers in silence.

"*What about your ghost?*"

On the drive down to Sugar Hill, Kathryn kept asking herself the same question. Had Rebeca really haunted her? Or had she simply been the invention of Kathryn's restless mind? A manifestation of Jack's "prompts?" A conjuring summoned by his Machiavellian scheme for revenge?

It was terrible what had happened to him. Witnessing a mother's murder, no matter how young one is, must leave traumatic residue that, even if forgotten or repressed, will metastasize eventually. The stuff of nightmares, surely. And then to discover one's entire worldview is a lie, that the surrogate father you believed had rescued you from your emotional wilderness was, in fact, the author of that very condition, well that must damage one's moral compass irreparably. But what good would be served dragging Jack's name through the mud now? Warren Wright had been the real villain here. Rebeca was his victim. And so was Jack.

And she had made a promise. Whether Rebeca's ghost existed didn't matter now. Kathryn would keep the secret of what he'd done. She'd protect Rebeca's little Jack-Jack. Justice had been served.

Almost.

There might be one other explanation. What if she had subconsciously invented an obsession with finding Rebeca's murderer to assuage her own guilt for what happened with Rex Baudry when she was a teenager? Had she succumbed to a subliminal urge to atone? Would bringing justice to Rebeca's murderer make up for her own mistake? Dr. Frankle was emphatic in her attempts to get Kathryn to forgive herself. Yes, she may have been sexually aggressive, Frankle would say, *click, click,* but Kathryn was *not* the architect of what happened. There was no gray area here. A grown man who surrendered his self-control to a girl, even a girl with a woman's body, was only using the myth of his own weakness to justify the unspeakable.

But what about *her* weakness?

The house was quiet and still. Sloane was at her weekly bridge game at The Cottages. The servants were in the kitchen preoccupied with plans for a dinner party that weekend, and the nurse had taken the opportunity of Kathryn's visit to indulge a long walk to the meadows to shed the stench of decay.

Kathryn fingered Rebeca's pistol in her jacket pocket as she went up the stairs, still surprised the police had returned it after they closed the case.

She sat by the bed in Rex's sick room, holding his pathetic stare for as long as she could. It would be so easy to rid herself of this decrepit reminder of her past. She could turn off his ventilator and he'd be gone in a matter of minutes, certainly before the nurse returned. Perhaps he would even urge her to do it, if he could. The Rex Baudry she remembered would have been terrified by this vision of himself. She pulled Rebeca's pistol from her pocket and put it on his bedside table to let him see a potential way out. She watched as his eyes drifted over to it. At first, she recognized the terror there, but after a moment, the fear dissolved and a kind of hopefulness replaced it. If he could have used the gun, Kathryn had no doubt the miserable son of a bitch would have. But he couldn't. And she wouldn't. She put the pistol back in her pocket. This was justice enough. His helplessness was the inescapable prison he deserved. She was almost ashamed to admit that she hoped he was conscious enough to understand his situation. And was suffering. But those thoughts evaporated as quickly as they'd emerged, and a kind of peace began to settle over her. It was as if the sudden breeze coming through the windows carried her anger and guilt away with it. She didn't care anymore. About him, about what happened between them. She left him there, wallowing in his incapacity and dissolution. He would have to live that way for whatever time he had left.

For the first time, Kathryn felt like she'd be able to do the same. She might never truly forgive herself as Dr. Frankle implored, but she'd be able to live with it. For the first time, she felt liberated.

She went downstairs and out the front door without saying goodbye to any of the servants. She left the door open and invited that healing breeze to escort her away.

The nurse was on her way back to the house and had a mildly perturbed expression when Rebeca's Mercedes passed by. Kathryn was leaving before she'd returned to her duty.

Kathryn nodded to her but got nothing in return.

She pulled out on to Route 17 and never looked back.

epilogue

Washington, DC

City of ghosts. For some, the Potomac sparkles with the lights of their monuments, their struggles memorialized, their accomplishments revered. For the rest, it's the purgatory of oblivion, the void of regret, where they linger, unfinished, unsettled.

Except for one, trapped here once upon a time, alone and helpless, in a charming Federal-style brick townhouse on Reservoir Road where cathedrals of elms that are lush in summer and gothically spare in winter shade the streets, where gracious family rooms with wainscoted walls and wide plank floors once murmured and sighed until another young woman arrived to help her pass through the veils of her desolation.

To find justice.

And finally, peace.

about the author

John Harrison began his career directing rock videos and collaborating with famed horror director, George Romero for whom he composed the scores to Romero's *Creepshow* and *Day of The Dead.* Harrison wrote and directed multiple episodes of Romero's classic TV series, *Tales From the Darkside* before helming *Tales From the Darkside, The Movie* for Producer Richard Rubinstein and Paramount Pictures which won Harrison the Grand Prix du Festival at Avoriaz, France. He has written and directed multiple TV episodes for a variety of networks as well as world premier TV movies and miniseries, including the two Emmy-winning miniseries adaptations of Frank Herbert's *Dune* and *Children of Dune* which he wrote, directed and co-produced. He co-wrote the Disney animated feature, *Dinosaur*, and wrote and directed the theatrical adaptation of Clive Barker's *Book of Blood.* Harrison's three-episode miniseries *Residue*, which he created and wrote, was a Netflix original. He is currently writing and directing episodes of the *Creepshow* TV series on Shudder/AMC, as well as writing/directing the new Universal Music Group/Treefort horror podcast, *FearWorm.*

If You Liked ...

If you liked *Passing Through Veils*, you might also enjoy:

Selected Stories: Horror and Dark Fantasy by Kevin J. Anderson

Mr. Menace by R. Michael Burns

Monsters, Movies, and Mayhem, Kevin J. Anderson, Executive Editor

other wordfire press
titles

Our list of other WordFire Press authors and titles is always growing. To find out more and to shop our selection of titles, visit us at:

wordfirepress.com